I0742574

HUMOR DEEPER THAN A HOLLER

LUCIUS MCCRAY

Copyright © 2019 Gary McPherson
Charlotte, North Carolina

All rights reserved. No parts of this book may be used or reproduced
by any means, graphic, electronic, or mechanical, including
photocopying, recording, taping or by any information storage
retrieval system, without the written permission of the publisher except
in the case of brief quotations embodied in critical articles and reviews.

This novel is a work of fiction. Names, characters, places, and
incidents are either products of the author's imagination or used
fictitiously. All characters are fictional, and any similarity to people
living or dead is purely coincidental.

Cover and interior by ebooklaunch.com

First, to my wife.
Thank you for putting up with my grousing when I write.

Dream Raven Editing.
Thank you for making my stories presentable.

Ebook Launch.
Without your cover designs and proofreading, this book
would not see the light of day.

My beta readers.
Your fresh perspectives and insights take my stories to the
next level.

My parents.
Thank you for summers in Blacksburg, Virginia, and moving
us to North Carolina from California. You have given me a
lifetime of down-home humor and fun.

Thank you to Lukus for so many good memories.
I wish you still lived near the homestead.

CONTENTS

BIRDS AND BIDDIES

Today started out like most days. I got my shower and made myself presentable before I walked in to see Darla. She was standin' in the kitchen makin' breakfast. I occasionally like to sneak in and watch her work. I think it's good for a man to appreciate how his wife looks and works, especially as we get up in years. That way I don't find myself takin' her too much for granted.

She was standin' there in her tight blue jeans and T-shirt. I love the way her thick wavy black hair falls halfway down her back. Despite our boys' best efforts, she still has all of her hair, unlike me. Judgin' from her outfit, she was plannin' to head out to the farm and tend to the hens, gather some eggs, and spend some time with her pet turkey. Lawd, how I do hate that turkey. Although, I have no doubt he'd be good eatin'.

Darla must've heard me thinkin' about dinner time with her turkey. She turned around, lookin' annoyed, and said, "Are you just going to stand there, or can you get the plates ready for me?"

I started to tell her I thought we should have Tom for dinner, but I was afraid she'd put that bird in a high chair and sit it right down at the table with the family. So, I decided to keep my mouth shut. I went ahead and got out our plates and got us both some much-needed coffee.

I have to say, there ain't nothin' more enjoyable than sittin' down to the breakfast table and enjoyin' the quiet of the early mornin'. Dependin' on the time of year, you'll see the countryside covered in a low layer of smoke from friends and neighbors runnin' their woodstoves and fireplaces to heat the cold mornings. In the summertime, you'll see a thin layer of clouds from the humidity that is just waitin' to heat up as the sun rises higher in the sky. Neither of those is much fun to be out workin' in, but they're sure pretty to look at.

Today was a smoky kind of day. Now by northern standards, we are downright mild, but by the standards of all the sane people in the world, we get a mite cold down this way a few weeks a year. This mornin' was down around freezin'. The cold air let that chimney smoke just hang across the yards in our neighborhood, and the air smelled like campfires with frost-covered grass glistenin' below the smoky hue.

Darla had made us eggs, grits, and bacon. She'd even thrown some bacon into the grits. At first, I was feelin' a little suspicious. Darla knows I love bacon and grits more than any other food for breakfast. Of course, puttin' bacon in grits is about as near to heaven as I dare to go on this side of livin'. Needless to say, I was wonderin' what occasion might warrant such a bountiful feast. I wanted to find out what was goin' on, but I didn't dare ask her outright. If she was just bein' nice and I questioned her motives, I wouldn't see bacon and grits again for at least a month.

I wiped my mouth free of coffee and bacon grease then smiled. Pushing my back into my chair, I stretched out my legs under the table, and said, "This is the best breakfast we've had in a long time. Did I forget my birthday or our anniversary?"

Darla laughed. "No, I just felt like being nice. You don't have any of your shine left from this fall. You've been working hard getting the farm ready for spring, and you took me to see our grandkids. I just thought it was time I do something for you."

She was convincin', but her lovin' compassion still felt out of character to me. Occasionally, Darla will recognize the things I try to do for her, but normally she repays me by lettin' me watch my TV shows in peace. She might even make me grits or bacon, but never both. This felt like a bribe or an apology. Still, I knew better than to press my luck.

"Thank you," I said. "This is downright motivatin' for me to do more."

Darla smiled. "I'm sure I can come up with something."

I worried what she meant by that.

I helped Darla get the dishes cleared off and got ready to head to the farm to check on the biddies for eggs and start workin' on the tractor.

I had hoped to start discin' a field in a few days, and the old girl was due for some maintenance before she hit the fields again. Normally, Darla joins me so she can visit with Tom. Did I mention that I can't stand the idea of some holiday meal being used as a pet? But I can't say no to my wife. To my surprise, she told me she would be headin' out later to the farm and that I should take care of things myself.

So, Wobbly and me headed on out. While I was takin' care of the eggs, Wobbly was walkin' and sniffin' all around the barn, chicken coop, and pretty much everywhere within eyeshot of me. I reckoned he was still worried about them coyotes. Fortunately, a few of us went out and got rid of two packs of them critters. The poor sheriff got bit by one that he thought was dead. He had reached down to turn it over, and it bit his hand. The good sheriff had to get rabies shots like I did. Bless his heart.

Anyway, Darla came rollin' up about an hour or so after I got there. Her car ain't too hard to spot. It's a pink Kia Soul. She had a special paint job done to get the right color pink. It sort of reminds me of a bottle of her nail polish rollin' down the road. Fortunately, she doesn't do much drivin' in it. The farthest she has taken her cosmetic on wheels is up to Columbia for some shoppin'. Unlike my pickup truck, which smooths out at eighty miles an hour, her car hums along at a nice sixty-five. Of course, she doesn't have the speeding tickets I do either. I don't know if that's because of the car's lack of speed or the fact that no officer wants to be seen next to it.

She got out of her oversized nail polish bottle on wheels and looked like she was dressed to go to town instead of workin' around the farm. She had changed into tan slacks, a black velvet laced blouse, and her white sweater. She looked plumb silly out here in the dirt, gravel, and dust.

She smiled, walked up to me, gave me a hug, and then said, "I'm takin' Tom to town with me."

Well, I was dumbfounded. I have heard some crazy ideas in my day, but takin' the turkey to town was about as thick as a bag of rocks at the bottom of a river. Of course, I'm not gonna say that to her, mostly on account of enjoyin' breathin' too much. Instead, I asked her, "Why?" Granted, that wasn't much of a question, but what can you say?

She told me in an excited voice, "You know my friend Bernice that owns the dog grooming place?"

I nodded because I was pretty sure I knew where this was goin', but I just couldn't imagine I was right.

"Well," she continued, "I was tellin' her how you won't allow Tom to stay at our house and how he gets real dirty out here on the farm. I asked her if she had ever considered groomin' a turkey. She said she had never heard of such a thing."

I couldn't hold back my laughter, and then interjected, "I reckon she hasn't."

Darla shot me a look that told me if I did that again I'd be sleepin' with Wobbly tonight, and then she kept talkin'. "Well, laugh if you want. I talked her into bathing Tom for me."

I put my hands up in front of me, took a step back, shook my head, and carefully said, "Hang on now, woman. Even if you have the money to get that turkey groomed, you don't know what he's gonna do when Bernice tries to bathe him. Tom is easily twenty-plus pounds. What if he hurts Bernice? We don't have the money to cover her medical costs. Not to mention the dogs waitin' their turn to get groomed—they'll kill Tom for sure."

Darla smirked and then shook her head. She put her hand on her hip, and said, "Lucius, do you think I'm that stupid? First of all, she is doing this on her day off. Second of all, I have agreed to help her bathe Tom this first time. Tom loves me and trusts me. Bernice has an apron I can put on to keep my clothes from getting dirty. She figures if we are successful she can have a farm animal day a couple times a month and charge more than she does for the dogs."

I couldn't hold back no longer, so I responded, "Darla, this is the craziest thing I done heard of. There ain't no farmer worth his salt going to pay to have his favorite cow or pig gussied up."

Darla started laughing at me, so I knew right then that there was somethin' I had missed. She always laughs if she knows she is gonna win an argument with me. Of course, I don't mind none. That woman's laughter can light up the whole farm. Although, I reckon I do wish I wasn't the source of so much of her joy.

Darla finally got control of herself, and said, "You are forgetting about the fairs and horse shows. We have 4-H, FFA, and breeders that show animals all the time. Some of those people need help, and they would be more than happy to pay someone who is good with animals and grooming."

Well, I knew she was right, and I had lost the argument, again. Of course, Tom was no show bird, and we weren't breedin' horses or any other kind of show animal. "How do you plan to pay to get ole Tom cleaned up?" I asked.

Darla reached in her purse and pulled out a wad of cash money. "With my Molasses money. You said that was mine, and I could spend it as I see fit."

Well, she had me. That woman not only was easy on the eyes but a hard worker to boot. She'd been making molasses for years and was right good at sellin' it. I can't remember a time when I could find full jars of molasses in the house on account of them all bein' sold. I suppose Darla has enough money hidden away that she could buy herself a new car if she really wanted to. Of course, that will never happen as long as she likes drivin' that pink nail polish bottle.

I slumped my shoulders. There wasn't anything else to say. Darla walked up and gave me one of the longest hugs and kisses we had done in years. I reckon if I had known I'd get that kind of reaction, I would've driven that stupid turkey to the groomer myself. She pushed herself back, and her eyes sparkled and danced.

I was beginin' to think we might go up to the hayloft, but then she said, "Can you go get Tom for me? I can't possibly get my clothes dirty, and he is filthy. Just put him in the back of the car."

Well, that certainly killed whatever mood we had goin' in the cool of the mornin'. I wasn't sure how much more indignity I could take. Of course, every time I do somethin' for that woman, she seems to find a way to give me a little more indignity, and I always seem to find a way to enjoy it. I was just happy my buddy Lukus was not around to see this. I would never hear the end of it.

I left Darla by the car and headed to the barn. We kept Tom in a horse stall at night. Thankfully, I hadn't let him out yet, or I'd be runnin' all over our field lookin' like an idiot tryin' to catch him.

Tom came struttin' up to the gate of the horse stall thinkin' he was finally gonna get out to run around. I wedged my body into the gap of the gate as I pulled it open. Tom backed up, a bit surprised by my change of habit.

Before he could figure out what was goin' on, I reached down and grabbed that old bird by the neck. You ain't never seen nor heard such squawkin' and hollerin'. His snood and wattle flopped around, loose feathers started fallin' out, and dust was just a flyin' off his dirty body. I finally manage to get my arm around his big ole body and get him subdued. Knowin' he was defeated, old Tom calmed down. I'm guessin' he thought he was goin' to be dinner.

I walked on out to Darla's cosmetic car and put Tom in the back seat. He started gobblin', but he was in no mood for a second round, so he stayed where I put him. Darla looked at my flannel shirt all covered in feathers and dirt and just shook her head. She carefully leaned in and gave me a peck on the cheek then headed down the farm road for town.

I looked down and saw Tom had left me a present down the side of my jeans. Since there wasn't nobody around but me, I said a couple words I knew I shouldn't and then head over to clean the chicken coop. Fortunately, I was already dirty. That was when it dawned on me that Wobbly hadn't been around offerin' to help with Tom. I looked around, and I couldn't find him anywhere. So, I started hollerin'.

I heard a faint noise at the edge of the woods and started walkin' that direction. A moment later, Wobbly popped out carryin' a dead skunk inside his massive jaws. I looked up to the sky and asked the good Lord what mischief I had done got myself into that I deserved such a mornin'. Wobbly was trying his best to get across that field. Lawd, he was a funny sight. A part of that skunk's body would get under one of his short legs and send Wobbly rollin'. He'd get up, pick the thing back up in his mouth, run a few feet, and do it all over again.

I figured he'd give up and leave it out there, and so I was standin' there just a laughin' every time Wobbly rolled over that skunk. It wasn't until he was halfway across the field that I quit laughin'. I could smell that dog at least a hundred yards away, and I realized he was intent on bringin' me that smelly dead varmint.

I started backin' up slowly. I figured I had a good head start on him, and the truck wasn't more than 150 feet behind me. He was movin' slow on account of him doin' summersaults every couple of feet.

I began a hollerin', "Wobbly, you idiot, drop that skunk! Leave it, boy! I don't want it!"

It was about this time I realized ole Wobbly doesn't understand a lot of English. He just kept flippin' and comin' my way.

"Drop that skunk now!" I started yellin' in a bit of a panic. To my relief, he stopped and dropped the dead animal. To my horror, he simply walked around it and began pullin' it backwards.

Now some folks may not realize this, but bulldogs were bred to control full-grown bulls. They grab hold of the ring in the bull's nose and can pull that bovine around anywhere you want 'em to. Even though Wobbly is only part bulldog, it appeared his reverse gear was a part of that breed. That dog must have been makin' up twice the ground he had been gaining flippin' over himself goin' forward.

So, I did the only thing I could think of. I turned tail and ran for my pickup. I was in the cab with the windows rolled up and the doors locked before Wobbly came backin' up the yard by the barn with his prize. He stopped and looked around for a moment. I reckoned he was confused about where I had run off to. For a moment, I thought I might get lucky and he'd head off with the critter and drop it off at the barn, but there was no such luck.

Instead, Wobbly simply went to the only thing he associated with me, my pickup. He came draggin' that stinkin' dead thing around and dropped it right at my driver's side door. He sat down, looked up, saw my head through the window, and let out a couple of loud barks. His tail and butt were just a twitchin' with pride. Then he sat down and waited for me to come out and congratulate him.

I refused to move from my spot for at least five minutes. I prayed to the Lord, cryin' and pleadin' to the Almighty to please remove that skunk, but nothin' happened. After five minutes, Wobbly began to look sad, and I felt like a real heel. That poor fella had gone through a lot to kill that stinkin' animal and bring it to me. I couldn't blame him for bein' himself.

I found a dirty rag from under my seat and covered my face. Then I slid out the passenger side of the truck. The smell wasn't as bad as I thought, least until I turned the left front corner of my pickup. That was when I got a full whiff. That old dirty rag couldn't do nothin' to stop that odor from comin' through. I was expectin' it though, so I didn't lose my breakfast.

With tears in my eyes, I walked over and petted Wobbly's stinkin' body. Then I walked over and dropped the tailgate on the truck. I took a deep breath of dust, oil, and skunk through my old rag, put the rag in my pocket, picked up Wobbly, and put him in the back of the pickup. I left the tailgate down so he wouldn't feel boxed in before we left. Wobbly ain't one for tryin' to jump from heights. His legs are so short he has trouble touchin' the ground as it is. He's smart enough to know any real height would harm his body if he were to try and jump from it.

Thankfully, the skunk didn't smell as bad. Wobbly had stayed away from breakin' those stink glands when he killed him. I got me a shovel and took that dead animal all the way back down to the woods again. I was just enjoyin' the fresh air walkin' back when I got downwind of Wobbly in the back of my pickup.

I put the tailgate up and headed on back to the house. Folks that were outside gave me dirty looks all the way home. I don't know if it was because they saw Wobbly in the back of the truck tryin' to look over the edge of the truck bed or if it was the smell. I honestly hadn't thought about how Wobbly would do in the cold wind sittin' in the truck bed. I just knew that smelly hound wasn't sittin' in the cab with me. When we got home, his ears, eyes, forehead, lips—pretty near his entire head—were covered in dried, half-froze doggy drool. I reckoned he had kept his mouth open and let the wind throw slobbers all over him the entire way home.

I got a hold of Wobbly and took him directly to the backyard. Now the only way to get rid of skunk is with hydrogen peroxide, bakin' soda, and dish detergent. So, I left Wobbly inside the newly fenced backyard while I put me together a batch. I sprayed the concoction all over him and let it break down that smell, and then I washed him off. After that, I did it again for good measure. It was too cool to leave him outside, but I wasn't sure how well the cleanin' took on account of it being on my clothes.

I took a gamble and let Wobbly inside, and then I stripped naked on the porch. You really can't appreciate how cool fifty degrees feels until you stand outside naked in it for a few moments. I took my frigid body on inside and took myself a hot shower. Once I was all squared away, I got the push broom and used it to pick up my stinkin' clothes off the patio, dropped them in the burn barrel out back, and set them on fire.

I had just sat down when Wobbly started barkin' and twitchin'. I knew that meant Darla was drivin' up the driveway. I looked outside for the nail-polish-mobile. To my surprise, Lukus had arrived. I normally don't see much of old Lukus in the fall on account of huntin' season. I hoped nothing bad had happened.

I opened the front door before he was halfway to the front porch, and Wobbly went shootin' out to meet him. Wobbly jumped up on Lukus's leg and then sort of rolled off and landed on his side or back before jumping up and doing it all over again. Lukus bent down and sniffed.

He stood up and asked, "Did he get into a skunk?"

I started shakin' my head. "Dag nab it. I thought I got that smell off of him."

Lukus let out a short laugh. "He doesn't smell like skunk. He smells like Palmolive."

I nodded my head. "Good. He killed a skunk down in the woods near the barn."

Lukus bent over and started lovin' on Wobbly and tellin' him what a good boy he was. I was tryin' not to get mad because Lukus doesn't always think ahead like most folks. I reckoned he didn't realize encouragin' Wobbly would only mean that dog would go skunk huntin' again the next chance he got. I managed to stop Lukus's well-intentioned mistreatment of my dog by invitin' him in for coffee.

I grabbed the two of us a mug, and we sat down in the two chairs closest to the fire roarin' inside our stone fireplace. Wobbly lay down between us, smellin' like freshly washed dishes. For a couple of minutes, neither of us said a word. I don't know what ole Lukus was thinkin', but I was just thankful to be done with my chores and that skunk. Of course, after a few more seconds, my curiosity got the better of me.

I turned to Lukus. "So, what brings you out to my parts? I figured you'd be huntin'."

Lukus nodded. "Yea, I thought I would be too. We had an incident with my eleven-year-old, and I couldn't leave the house until a few minutes ago. It's too late for morning hunting. So, I thought I would drop by and say hello."

Now Lukus doesn't let anything get in the way of huntin' season, so I figured it must be serious. "Is Denise alright?"

Lukus nodded. "She's okay for an eleven-year-old. I'm afraid she may be upset for a while. She accidently killed Carol's prized hen."

Now, Carol loved that bird more than Darla loves her turkey. Lukus put up with it because Carol's fowl was a hen that laid eggs. She had also won best of show at the county fair. So, primpin' up that chicken was somewhat justified. I just couldn't imagine what Carol's response must have been.

I asked Lukus, "What happened? Did Carol tan Denise's hide?"

Lukus slowly shook his head. "No, she was a lot more understandin' than I would have thought she'd be."

I was plumb confused. "Tell me what happened. I can't imagine Carol bein' okay with her daughter killin' her bird."

Lukus sighed and put his coffee down on the small table between our chairs. He stretched out his legs and then turned towards me before beginning his tale. "Well, Lucius, you know that hen of Carol's was always a bit uppity after winning the county fair ribbon. I suppose Carol washing her, primping her, and what have you got to that birdbrain."

I nodded because I could relate.

Lukus continued, "Well, she started pecking at me in the mornings when I would try and get any eggs she had laid. So, I started taking the old biddy to the pond there in the back and dipping her head when she did it. Now it wasn't anything different than Carol would do when she was washing her. I wasn't abusing the spoiled fowl, but I wanted her to understand that pecking me was not allowed, no matter how many ribbons she won."

Lukus paused to finish off his coffee. I sat there stone silent, wonderin' where Denise worked into this.

Lukus put down his mug. "What I didn't know was that our daughter had been watching me. She's older now, so it never occurred to me that she would try to mimic anything I do. Well, last night, she got the idea into her head that she was going to surprise me with fresh eggs with dinner. She went out in the dark, and of course, that hen has nestled in for the night. Denise goes reaching underneath that bird, and the startled hen does what any of them would do in that situation. She pecks at her arm. Denise decided she would follow her daddy's example and grabs that bird by the neck and walks it down to the pond and holds its head under the water. Except, she didn't know when to bring its head up."

Lukus paused for a moment. I got to admit, I was on the edge of my seat. That poor child, killin' her momma's prized hen. I couldn't imagine the guilt that youngin' must have been feelin'.

Lukus started back up again, "Denise comes in the house balling her eyes out. She tells us what's happened. Carol goes running out the door, and I follow her. Sure enough, there's that old hen flopped over next to the water. I try pushing against that fowl, and some water comes streaming out of its mouth. So, I do it a few more times until there isn't any water left. I still couldn't get it to revive. However, seeing I had made some headway inspired me to try something. I figured I might be able to shock it awake. So, I ran to my shed and grabbed a bucket of cold water that should have been near freezing due to the cold nights."

I interrupted Lukus, "Do you mean to tell me that you were going to throw water on a bird that drowned?"

Lukus scowled. "I wasn't going to pour it in its mouth, just throw it on its body. I thought the shock of the cold water might revive it. What I didn't know was that Carol had put gasoline in the bucket to use for priming the old tractor engine that morning. I realized the switch when I smelled the fuel in the air as it spread across that bird's body. To our surprise, that hen jumped up and started running around the yard."

I was in shock. Lukus's stupid idea actually worked. I began to wonder if we could use moonshine and get the same result. "So, the hen's okay then?"

Lukus shook his head sadly. "I'm afraid not."

"Did it die?" I quietly asked.

"No," said Lukus somberly. "It ran out of gas."

I groaned at Lukus's horrible joke, and Wobbly growled. I reckon that dog does know more English than I gave him credit for. I shook my head. "You had me goin' for a minute there."

Lukus answered emphatically, "I'm not jokin'. The biddy flopped around something awful before she finally died."

"Goodness, how are Carol and Denise? Is your wife even talkin' to your daughter?"

Lukus nodded. "Yea, the two are getting along as well as can be expected. Carol doesn't blame Denise, and Denise feels just awful, but we are trying to make the best of it. That's why I came over. We are having skinless grilled chicken, and I wanted to see if you and Darla would like to come over for lunch."

"Darla isn't here," I said, feelin' relieved, but I could not leave well enough alone. "Isn't that gas inside the bird now? I'd expect that would be dangerous eatin'."

Lukus shook his head. "That's why it's skinless. I put that bird on the grill as soon as we had the feathers plucked and the bird gutted. That skin went up like the fourth of July. You've never heard such sizzling and popping. The rest of the meat should be done soon. You're welcome to come alone if you like."

"I'll pass," I said with a smile. "I need to be here when Darla gets back from town. We have some chores around here to finish up." I didn't have the heart to bring up Tom's turkey spa.

Lukus shrugged. "Suit yourself, friend. I better head on back and help Carol get lunch on the table."

I saw Lukus out and came back inside the house. I had just finished my nap in front of the fireplace when I heard the distinct sound of a turkey gobblin' in my front driveway. This time I knew it had to be Darla. I guess Wobbly knew too because he was barkin' and bumpin' his body hard up against the door.

I worked my way out the front door while maneuverin' to keep the dog and the turkey apart. I finally got out the front door. Darla had that silly bird on some kind of leash and was tryin' to wrestle it up to the house. I walked over, gave Darla a kiss, and picked up the irate fowl. Darla looked a little shocked at my initiative and handed me the leash when I held out my hand. I took the useless contraption off the fowl. I may not appreciate Tom as a pet, but even animals condemned to be eatin' deserve more dignity than Tom had been given.

I carried him to the backyard, put him down, closed the gate, and walked into the house through the back door. Darla was standing there next to the fire with her coat off.

"Are you planning on making Tom stay out in the cold?" she asked in a tone of disgust.

I nodded. "Well, at least its grass, so Tom won't get as dirty. I'll let him sleep in the laundry room at night so he won't get too cold."

Darla's expression relaxed. "Thank you, sweetheart," she said as she walked up and gave me another one of those kisses I enjoy.

After she released my lips, I decided I'd bring up the one problem with our arrangement. "You do realize if we want to go out we'll have to get a sitter. We can't leave Wobbly and Tom in the backyard alone together."

Darla leaned up against the kitchen counter and nodded. "I hadn't thought about that. Who on earth would sit for a dog and turkey?"

"What about Denise?" I offered. "Lukus's daughter is good with animals."

Darla's face lit up. "I love that idea. I'll call over there right now."

I quickly interjected, "Not right now, dear. I mean, we ain't goin' nowhere right now anyway. I'll call Lukus on Friday and ask about the weekend. After all, the girl's only eleven. It ain't like she's datin' yet."

"Okay," said Darla. "Why don't you enjoy some television while I make us lunch?"

"I like that idea," I said as I headed for my favorite chair.

I had just flipped on the screen when Wobbly walked over and lay down so he was facing me. I swear that dog had the biggest smile I'd ever seen. Maybe that canine really does know more English than any of us can imagine. In any case, we both had a wonderful afternoon.

BEACH AND BAR

M ost folks picture us country boys in the mountains with bare feet and our stills boilin' up some good down-home brew. Some of y'all might even picture me with a straw hat and denim overalls. Well, that last part might be true some of the time. There ain't nothin' better than a good pair of overalls for workin' in, but I don't know anybody who works all the time. Shoot, I ain't out workin' unless I have to. Which I suppose is why most folks picture people in the country as lazy. I feel bad for people like that. They don't realize that your life is mighty short, and you need to smell God's good roses every chance you get.

Now, I lived that city life for a lot of years. It's hard livin' on account of people focusin' more on workin' themselves to death than enjoyin' the privilege of breathin'. I moved into the concrete jungle on account of there bein' money to be made. Unfortunately, a lot of money has to be spent for the privilege of livin' the city life. After all, somebody must pay for them skyscrapers, asphalt, and concrete.

The air's dirty, and the water tastes funny, but there is still a lot of prestige that comes with livin' in the city. I suppose that's because folks assume women in dress suits and men in tailored suits must be workin' hard. After all, only an idiot would want to wear them things all the time for fun. They are a pain to get on and a pain to wear and a pain to keep up.

In reality, most folks in them uptown buildings did nothin' but spend half their day jawin' to one another about their friends, television shows, or who was cheatin' on their spouse with another co-worker. At least in the country we stay busier than a one-legged man in a butt kickin' contest when there is work to be done.

Down on the farm, we don't stop workin' 'til the chores are done, but then we have more fun than a tub full of PJ. That's because we play as hard as we work. For example, I spent half my summer puttin' together an old truck from junk pieces of tractors and vehicles that were rustin' around the farm. Then this winter, me and the boys had us a few truck races up in the mud, ice, and through the woods. Of course, by the time we got done racin' my truck was just junk again, but I don't know anybody that doesn't like to run the wheels off of a truck in the woods.

By contrast, most city folk think standin' around and drinkin' watered-down liquor is a good time. When they want to get real crazy, they'll pay some fella to take perfectly good music and interrupt it with somethin' that sounds like a cat gettin' skinned, and then they repeat the same measure of music over and over, and those highfalutin' folks try to dance to it. Truth be told, the women normally do a pretty good job of dancin', but the men just sort of twitch in place while holdin' their watered-down alcohol.

So, it should come as no surprise that I like to do somethin' besides drinkin' when I want to have a good time. My favorite way of relaxin' is travelin'. My favorite destination is some beach somewhere. Now, you've probably seen some country singer with a picture of him or herself with their cowboy hat on down yonder in Myrtle Beach or maybe even Daytona, but that ain't how most of us look.

No, you find most Carolina boys down at the beach with a base-ball cap. Some of us may even be sportin' a Bermuda hat to keep our red necks a little less red. If it's cold, we got no issues with wearin' jeans or slacks along the beach. We just avoid the water because we're smart enough not to get our long pants wet in the cold. If you ever see people wadin' in the water when it's fifty degrees, it's because they're Yankees. People from up north don't have the sense to know that you shouldn't go into the water when it's colder than seventy-five degrees.

Now, I've been over yonder to the West Coast and their beaches. You always see these beautiful women layin' out mostly naked in the sand, and the boys all playin' volleyball or guitars. Some of those fellas can even do both. Leastwise, that's how the movies show it, and they make the movies out there, so I reckon they ought to know. I will say when I visited out there I didn't see none of that.

Most of the time, you'll see their surfboards sittin' on the sand instead of in the water. I found out right quick why they don't spend too long ridin' the waves. It's because the water out there is so dang cold there ain't nobody wantin' to swim in it without a wetsuit. That's how the locals out west can tell who's a tourist without even speakin' to 'em.

The tourists are the ones standin' around shiverin' in the cold water. That usually precedes them trying to body surf, or boogie board, and instead getting a mouthful of seawater when a wave crashes down on them. Of course, there are exceptions to my perception. Younger local teenagers and small children swim in the California ocean on account of them not havin' the good sense to get out when they're cold.

There is a plus side to this cold water though. They don't have near as many critters as we do over here on the East Coast. I heard there are great white sharks out in those cold waters, but I didn't ever see any. I imagine if they are in those waters, those fish ain't gonna bother anybody. They're too busy swimmin' so they can keep warm. Of course, if a tourist happens to be swimmin' in their path, it would probably get interestin'. Then again, they get so many tourists in California, I'm not sure anybody would notice if one went missin'.

Now down here in the Southeast, our water is warm. Well, least-wise it's warm in the summer and most of the fall when folks want to be at the beach. In the summertime, if you ain't at the beach you're in the house praying the air conditioner don't break. Now, the fall is downright pleasant, and it feels a lot like California did, except our water is a lot more comfortable.

Unfortunately, it don't do folks no good to lay out on a Carolina beach in the fall. Everyone that tries it either ends up as red as a lobster, or they look as pale as they did when they showed up on the coast. Usually the lobsters are from up north. They don't have the good sense to get out of the sun just because the weather is good. The pale folks are the locals who decide laying on the sand all day ain't a good use of their time, and so they don't spend much time lying around. They either get in the water or go shoppin'. Once you get out of that water, you realize it may not be as warm as you thought, so you go shoppin' anyway.

I realize that may not sound like a good time to everybody, but that's because you ain't tried it yet. In the summertime, that eighty-degree water feels cooler than the air. Although, I do have to admit the humidity drippin' in the summer air normally feels just as wet as the water.

As for places folks go when they want to play in the water, Wrightsville beach up near Wilmington comes to mind. It's a beautiful location with hotels and houses for rent everywhere. Normally, you'll find the locals stayin' in the beach houses because they either own them or have a buddy that tells them what house to rent. The Yankees and city folks enjoy the resorts. The high prices and crowded restaurants make them feel important. In addition, it helps the local economy, so everybody is happy with the arrangement.

Wrightsville Beach even gets some pretty decent waves, for the Atlantic Ocean. Of course, all that wave action causes riptides, so the beaches are normally pretty excitin' during the tourist season in the Carolinas. Now folks out west have riptides too, but they ain't near as bad. Out yonder in California, their beaches go out a few feet and then the ground just sort of falls away. I reckon if folks saw how far they were above the ground, most of 'em would be afraid to go into the water.

Down east, we have all kinds of sand. You can walk out yonder for yards and yards. Even if a fella can't touch ground, he can keep swimmin' until he does. Unfortunately, all that sand movin' around the waves forms some pretty deep troughs, and the next thing you know you have swimmers getting' sucked out to the ocean like gas through a pump. Fortunately, the water is so shallow the locals don't get in trouble too often, just tourists. There's always some fella or woman with their nose covered in sunscreen out in the water with no floatin' device getting saved by the lifeguards. Some folks down 'round those parts just consider that entertainment.

That may sound a bit harsh, but there's a reason some locals become callous. Every night the news tells about someone drownin' or a swimmer who had to be saved from the rip currents. The beaches here have flags up when the riptides are bad. I suppose some tourists figure it ain't fair that they need to stay out of water after spendin' all their money and time to come down to the beach, and so they go swimmin' anyway. It makes about as much sense as playin' on a high-way. Still, I have to respect city folks who would rather swim in a rip current than stand around drinkin' watered-down liquor in the city.

Besides our rip currents, there are a few other things you have to look out for on our beautiful coastlines. We have an abundance of sharks, stingrays, crabs, and jellyfish. None of these critters are really people-friendly. Now it may sound funny, but I like goin' to the beach to see the critters. There's somethin' beautiful about standin' on the beach and seein' a school of fish swimmin' inside a wave. It's too bad that normally means there are sharks nearby. How do I know that's true? Well, if you go to the beach during low tide near Wilmington, North Carolina you're liable to find baby sharks swimmin' in the tidal pools durin' the summer.

Needless to say, there are a heap of things goin' on at the beaches in the Southeast. That's why most of the time Darla and I go in the off-season, which normally falls between November and May. During that time, most of the Yankees quit comin' down because they are busy talkin' in their cubicles, and the beaches and communities in the Carolinas take on a much more relaxed vibe. Of course, you ain't gonna be walkin' 'round in shorts when you're there on the off-season. Here in the Carolinas, we can be seventy-one degrees one day and forty degrees the next during any time of year other than summer. So, when we go in the off-season, we are always careful to pack slacks and shorts.

Unfortunately, durin' the cooler months you don't find as many live critters near the beach, but you do find their skeletons, or shells. You also have a fair chance of seein' a dolphin or two. Without the Yankees in the water, them dolphins have no issue with cruisin' the coastline lookin' for food. If you time it just right, you may even see a shark, normally being followed by dolphins.

Since the kids are in school, most places are cheaper to visit and a whole lot quieter. Many of the tourists you're likely to find are retirees who don't care much for other folks' youngsters havin' a conniption fit out in the sand. I can't blame them none. After all, older folks have raised their kids and want peace and quiet in their golden years.

Now that Darla and I are into the silver years of our marriage together, we decided to take us a trip to the beach to celebrate our anniversary. With school in session, we weren't liable to run into any cryin' rug rats by the sea, or teenagers goin' hog wild at night.

Although Carolina weather is always a gamble, it was plumb beautiful even if it was a mite on the cool side. The sky was a Carolina blue during the day, and an even prettier North Carolina State red during the sunsets. The only problem was the wind. Here in the Carolinas, our wind gets confused about when it should appear and where it should come from. We normally get windy days when the temperature is a tepid fifty-five degrees or so. That normally feels like it's in the forties. In the summertime, we can't buy wind most days. So, when it's ninety degrees and humid, it feels like it's in the hundreds. Every Southerner I know has asked the good Lord to turn that around, but so far, He just keeps sayin' no. I reckon it's on account of Him havin' a sense of humor that us mere mortals can't understand.

Darla and I went out our first afternoon to do us a bit of beach combin'. The good Lord never changes, and He gave us a right breezy fifty-degree day. It was blowin' out of the north, so that wind felt as cold as a frosted frog. Headin' south on the beach with the wind felt a mite warmer than walkin' north. Unfortunately, we had to walk north to get back to our hotel. On the plus side, we were able to find us a few decent shells since most folks with common sense were avoidin' the beach on account of the cold wind.

Darla and I stayed out there long enough to get sand in our beach shoes and spray from the water that left us feeling even chillier than when we started. I had thought ahead though since we do this sort of thing every year. I got us a right nice hotel room facing the ocean. I figure if you're goin' to the beach, you should be stayin' on the beach.

So, we sat inside and warmed up while we enjoyed watchin' the waves. We even saw a couple of surfers in wetsuits come out and try their luck since the wind was kickin' up powerful lookin' swells. It looked like those wetsuit-clad beach bums hadn't seen waves that big before, and so they'd either missed every wave or just plumb fall over.

I suppose some could argue sittin' in a room watchin' the beach is about as excitin' as twitchin' to that club music. I reckon I can't argue with that. Although sittin' and watchin' surfers wipe out in the cold water is free. Those bar tabs can run up higher than a hotel room, and you still have to go home at the end of the night. Clubbin' aside, that first day was downright relaxin', if not a tad chilly.

When dinner time came, we thought we'd go to a place we'd been to before called Sharky's. The place has a lot of atmosphere and a right decent bar. Even though it was the off-season, we still had to wait for a table. They invited us to go to the bar and have a drink while we waited. That bar was packed plumb to the gills. There was an NC State basketball game on the flat screens. Given that's where Darla and I met while we were attendin', we both enjoyed the game while we shared us a rum runner.

We stood there, soakin' up the atmosphere. The restaurant has older lookin' boards and faded paint that gives it that real seaside kind of a feel. I reckon part of that may be because it's on Ocean Isle, and they're next to the Intracoastal Waterway. Lookin' around the bar, I saw all sorts of regalia. There were funny license plates from around the nation, fishin' nets, surfboards—all sorts of eclectic knickknacks were around that buildin'. I could just imagin' the stories behind 'em as I stood in the sea of bodies waitin' to hear my name over the drone of conversations. That place was busier than a moth in a mitten.

Then this group of girls walked into the bar to wait on their table. Now, I get in trouble sometimes for callin' women girls, but when you're my age, anyone under thirty still looks like a kid. Part of this is on account of them lookin' so young and fit while I'm lookin' a mite flabby and wrinkly. The other reason has to do with experience. The older the good Lord allows us to get, the more we realize we don't know how the world works. We look back at our youth and admit that we couldn't have hit the ground if we had thrown ourselves at it.

Well, these young women were dressed to the nines. I turned to Darla and said, "It must be a bachelorette party 'cause they are way overdressed."

Lookin' around the room, anyone could see the locals were wearin' jeans, T-shirts, sweatshirts, and ball caps—and that was the women.

Then here were these young ladies in fashionable black, pink, and blue dresses. You'd a thought they were lost.

The only thing Darla did was nod to my comment on account of it being so loud. There were around ten or so girls of various persuasions. They were the sort of girls that could make a fella miss his younger college days. I found myself wonderin' what their stories were. Why would such finely dressed young ladies come to this shanty styled bar and grill on a dark, cold night? After all, North Myrtle Beach and Myrtle Beach were just down the road and even in the winter time the nightlife there gives people their age somethin' to enjoy.

All of a sudden, one of the girls spoke up. She didn't yell, but her voice cut through the din of folks visitin', it cut through the basketball game, and then it cut right through my skull. I looked over at her, and to my surprise, it was the girl I thought was the bride-to-be. Although her voice had the ability to cut through steel, it was still tough to make out all her words.

All I heard was, "Hi everyone, we are the...club from UNC!"

Now that right there got my attention. Darla and I went to NC State. UNC is our bitter rival for more reasons than I can write down in a simple short story. Back in the 1980s when we roamed The Brickyard, I often changed the meaning of UNC. UNC is, of course, the University of North Carolina. Some folks add Chapel Hill on the end of that on account of the location of the campus. Students from the school, or its rivals, drop the town name. That's partly to give the devil his due. There is only one real UNC, so you don't need to be puttin' in its town. Now, when I was a student, I often referred to it as the University of No Class. Students at UNC normally referred to us as hillbillies and engineers. I suppose they thought that was an insult.

I also have friends who married UNC girls back in the eighties. That was on account of NC State being mostly boys and the Carolina girls lookin' for real men. So, my mind was awash with all sorts of thoughts as the drama began to unfold.

Here was this young lady with the guts to interrupt a large group of strangers, and I assumed it had to do with a weddin' party from UNC.

"We are goin' to sing a song for you," she said through her impressively loud mouth.

The next thing I knew, the women broke out in a chorus, and they sounded like angels. Amazingly, everyone got real quiet on account of them bein' so good. Although they sounded like angels, the words they were singin' wasn't nothin' angelic. It was about spendin' the night with a boy, and let me tell you, I got tore up inside. I went from bein' embarrassed, to bein' intrigued, to wishin' I was younger, to feelin' guilty. Middle age is a bit like middle school. You're young enough to remember what it's like to be young, but your body is getting' older. You have no idea what to do about it, and you know you have to keep movin' on.

So, while I was tryin' not to listen and look, I started watchin' folks around the room. I have to be honest; I watch and listen to folks all the time, on account of them givin' me ideas for my stories. I spied me a group of college-age boys lookin' at the girls and noticed the ladies were lookin' back at them. I began smilin' because I was happy for these boys. When they'd first decided to come to this establishment, they'd had no idea how good their night was going to get, but then to my amazement, they all pulled out their smartphones. Now, I assumed they were goin' to start filmin' these young ladies, but I was sadly mistaken.

The boys opened up one of those apps that somehow show you people in the room. I saw them there gigglin' over their phones and swipin' pictures left and right. It took all of my self-control not to walk over and slap them so hard in the back of their heads that their eyeballs would pop out of the front of their skulls. I was embarrassed for them. Here were these attractive young ladies rattling the walls with their fine voices. Their seductive song was being sung right at these young men, and those stupid boys looked at their cell phones. One thing is for sure, if this is how boys think the dating ritual works, birth control companies are goin' to go out of business followed by the human race.

Well, the girls finished the song and then holler, "Go Heels." That's Carolina's emblem, the Tarheel. It goes back to a time when North Carolina exported a lot of tar or pine pitch. Folks who go to NC State believe it ain't tar on their heels on account of all the bovines roamin' around in open fields. Of course, we're just a bunch of hillbillies who know how to walk across a cow pasture. Needless to say, I had to bite my tongue when I heard those girls holler for their school. Lookin' around the room, I wasn't the only one. I reckon that's because eastern North Carolina is normally populated by pirates—East Carolina's mascot—or wolves, which is North Carolina State's. So, their exuberance for their college fell a bit flat.

I had to give it to the young women; they were not deterred. They were still all grins and excitement as the hostess then led them to the dining room. Darla and I shook our heads in disapproval at the young men still busy on their phones. I guess their mommas never explained that givin' all their attention to their smartphones would only succeed in getting them hooked up with their phone when they're lookin' for companionship. Thankfully, I didn't have to suffer through their embarssin' stupidity for much longer. We were called to our table just a few minutes after the UNC serenade.

Most folks don't realize this, but I've never been one to seek out attention among strangers. To me, there is a difference between fellowshippin' with friends, relatives, or co-workers and being put into the midst of strangers. So, when we were put at the table in the center of the room near the dining room entrance, I wasn't sure where I wanted to sit 'cause there was no place to hide. I looked across from our table, and there sat that large group of young singers. I was now stuck between a rock and a hard place. If I sat on one side, the girls would be behind me, and they were as loud waitin' on their food as they were singin'. On the other side, I'd be sittin' near the doorway, but it would be a little quieter. So, I took the quiet side.

Now, Darla and I prefer our fish to come from the pasture instead of the sea. Thankfully, Sharky's had a fair number of menu choices. Now, if you ain't never been in eastern North Carolina, let me give you some good advice. There are two food types that part of the state excels in. One is fish, and the other is BBQ pork. Since I wasn't goin' to eat the fish, I opted for the pork. They brought it out on a large platter, and my mouth started waterin' so hard I had to work at swallowin' to stop the waterfall of saliva that was tryin' to form on my lip.

The golden pork and eastern sauce sat beneath a small pile of red coleslaw. I was able to see this because the large bun was overflowing with the goodness of an eastern Carolina BBQ sandwich. I lifted the pillowy soft buns that nestled my bite of pork ecstasy. The wonderful rich tangy flavor had just touched the tip of my grateful tongue when an ungodly high pitch reached into my eardrum and pierced through it like a knife through butter. I had to put down my sandwich and hold my right ear on account of the pain. I honestly thought my ear had started bleedin'.

My body tightened up, and I looked past Darla at the source of my agony. All the girls were laughin' and slappin' the table. Well, it was more like screechin' and slappin'. I ain't never heard such a racket. Please don't misunderstand me. This wasn't some Wolfpack vs. Heels sort of a moment. These women were honest to goodness screechin' like cats in a room full of rockin' chairs. I still don't know how such horrible sounds could come out of people with such beautiful voices. I looked over at Darla, and she was holdin' both her ears while wearing this pained look. Thankfully it only lasted a few seconds, although it felt like minutes.

Well, I went back to enjoyin' my sandwich when one of the boys workin' at the restaurant came over and started talkin' with the girls. I smiled because I thought there might be hope for the human race after all. Darla noticed and asked me why I was happy. Of course, I could have been smart and told her I was thinkin' about us, but instead, I decided to tell her the truth. I knew she would appreciate what I was seein', and I was right. Unfortunately, this young fella had some game in him. The next thing I know, he's got these girls a screechin' again, and this didn't happen just one time. They'd screech, and he'd laugh. Then they'd talk long enough for him to think of somethin' witty, and they'd start back up screechin' again.

Darla and I were torn. On the one hand, we wanted to get out of there, but on the other we were hungry, and Sharky's food was some of the best we'd enjoyed in a long time. We decided we'd be smart and eat slowly. After all, those young ladies had a long trip back to campus, so we knew they wouldn't stay long. So, it sort of became a game. We'd take a bite; they'd screech, and we'd stop eatin'. They'd simmer down, and we'd get another bite of food. This game slowed our eatin', and my stomach was not happy about having to wait.

Well, I noticed the girls finished eatin' fairly quick, just like I had predicted. Their suitor came back by, and I heard him say somethin' about the meal being free on account of them singin' in the bar. That seemed fair. These women did have beautiful singing voices, but they couldn't laugh worth a cent. As soon as I saw them start to stand up, I took a huge bite of my sandwich. I was a man on a mission, and that mission was to give in to my gluttony for that fine pork that had been teasing my tongue for the past ten minutes.

All of a sudden, from behind me I hear a familiar voice of that same young lady from before. Her voice cuts through the whole establishment this time, "Excuse me."

Now, I didn't turn around. I assumed they were standing between the bar and the dinin' room in the entry and exit pathway when the girl announced they were goin' to sing, "Killer Queen" by the band Queen. Now, I am a fan of that song, and I know those vocals are no small task, especially acapella.

I take another big bite as they start the song, and I have to say, they sounded so beautiful Freddie Mercury probably sat up in his grave to hear them, but then I noticed someone out of the corner of my eye. One of these attractive young ladies was standin' no more than a foot away from me. That was when I realized we were in the middle of their show. I tried chewin' down my big ole bite as fast as I could. That was when I notice all the cell phones out with people filmin' these young girls, and of course, us because our table was right there with them.

Well, I was fit to be tied. Here were all these cameras, and I had no place to run. Because of where Darla sat, she managed to keep her face away from most of the cameras. At least my head had gotten a little sunburned during our time out on the beach earlier in the day. If it hadn't, folks might have missed how embarrassed I was. Fortunately, with the sun-assisted hue, I lit up like a red Christmas bulb.

At this point, I did the only thing I could think of. I stared down at the remains of my BBQ sandwich. Part of me wanted to cry on account of my lukewarm sandwich of pork paradise sittin' a third of the way eaten and now lookin' a little sad. Part of me wanted to turn and watch those pretty girls sing, even if I did have to look at the ceiling to see some of their faces. One final part of me wanted to stand up screamin' and then run out of Sharky's.

I suppose if the food had not been so good, I might have gone with that last option, but I wanted to come back to Sharky's one day, and I reckoned they wouldn't allow me back through the front door if I ran out screamin' without payin' for my food.

I don't remember much after that moment. I do remember enjoyin' the music, and the sense of relief I had when they quit and finally left. But by then our dinner was in a sad state, and Darla and I were both still hungry. Although the food had gotten cold, it still tasted right decent. We were sad though, as both Darla and I were sure our anniversary meal would have far exceeded good at its original temperature.

Thankfully, the rest of the trip was peaceful. We enjoyed the Christmas shop in Calabash, and we found us a mess of seashells by the seashore to take home. The day we left for home was cloudy and cold. I appreciated the good Lord waitin' until we left to turn the weather gray. So, if you ever make your way to Ocean Isle, NC be sure and walk on the beaches and find yourself some pretty seashells, and by all means, grab a bite to eat at Sharky's. Just insist they put you at a table next to the wall.

BEARS AND BEER

My best buddy Lukus and I like to go running off without the womenfolk every now and then. A few years ago, he built himself a nice little cabin on the side of Roan Mountain, Tennessee. It's a beautiful place that was built around a couple of trees growing out of the mountainside. Now, when I say around a couple of trees, I mean he built that cabin plumb around two tree trunks. I reckon Lukus figured the trees worked like columns to hold the home in place on the cliff. I never have had the heart to ask him what he would do if those trees start dyin' and those roots break loose in a nasty rain storm. I try not to worry Lukus about such things unless the moment calls for it.

Don't get me wrong; it ain't no tree house. In fact, most of it sits below the road and driveway. You're liable to miss it if you ain't watching real close for the turnoff. The only thing you can see from the road is its roof and a mess of trees and bushes. However, when you walk inside, it's a downright pleasant surprise. There's a right decent entryway and a fair-sized livin' room. The tongue and groove floorin' and ceilin' look right smart. Lukus did a fine job puttin' it together. From the living room, it's a straight shot over to a small dinette and kitchen. I like sleepin' on the couch when we head up there, so it's a real convenient walk to the coffee in the kitchen. Next to the kitchen is the master bedroom and bath. Lukus put in a cathedral ceilin', and he built a loft over top of the bedroom, so you can fit in even more friends for the night when there's a big shindig. The wall lookin' out away from the mountain is made up of nothin' but windows. You can see out over the valley and onto the mountain ranges of North Carolina. On a good day, you can see Table Rock while you're havin' your mornin' brew.

Now, Lukus calls that view his Tennessee view, but there ain't nothin' Tennessee about it. You're lookin' at North Carolina. In the springtime and summer, the hillsides are covered in a menagerie of dark green, light green, and every shade in between green. The barns around the farms in the valley below dot the green landscaping with reds or grays, depending on their age. The fall is downright beautiful with it patchwork of reds and yellows in the forest.

Down yonder in the basement is even more room. That secret space holds two more small bedrooms, another bathroom between them, and a right cute playroom. It's not a huge place, but it's just right for a couple of fellas who want to get away from the hustle and bustle of life's responsibilities. The wall downstairs is covered in glass just like up yonder. However, the view ain't nearly as good on account of the tree line risin' up past the ground floor.

Of course, the isolation of the cabin is all Lukus and I really cared about. If you needed to get away and think or reflect, this was the ideal place. Lukus and I had a fella up there with us once, and he asked what we do. We smiled and broke open some beers. I handed that fella one and sat down in one of the many rocking chairs on that back deck. We put our feet up on the railin' and just looked out at the view. He kept complainin' and tellin' us how borin' things were.

Lukus and I must have been of the same mindset because we both turned around and said, "That's the idea."

I reckon that fella still hasn't learned how to relax.

Well, the itch had hit me to head on up to Lukus's mountain paradise, so I gave him a call, and we made plans to go on up that direction. I should mention that I could invite myself because Lukus and me are like brothers. I wouldn't recommend you just call any old acquaintances and start invitin' yourself to their vacation hideaways.

You may be wonderin' at this point what Darla thought about me headin' off on such excursions without her. Darla, as always, encouraged me to go. After all, it was a vacation for her too. Raisin' four sons meant she was around boys and men twenty-four hours a day, seven days a week. Even with the kids out of the house, she still had to deal with me walkin' around and getting' in the way of her day.

With Darla's blessing, and Lukus wantin' to get away as badly as I did, we were all set.

Needless to say, I wasn't surprised in the least bit when I came in from the farm the day before Lukus and I were plannin' to leave and found all my bags packed. Darla had even slipped in a small amount of moonshine that we could use either for ourselves or for the outside fireplace. I could not wait. I had needed some time away to think about the upcoming spring and just reflect on all the good God had given us lately.

The next day, Lukus was at my door. Darla had me a mug of coffee ready. I kissed her goodbye, petted Wobbly, wiped dog slobbers off my hand, and headed on out. Now if you ain't ever had a chance to see a Carolina spring mornin', I recommend you make the trip. Trees and plants were in bloom everywhere. Up here in North Carolina, they even plant flowers in the highway medians, so everywhere you look there are bright beautiful colors and all sorts of interestin' pollen. It's beautiful to look at, but it can really be murder if you have allergies.

I once had a doctor tell me that spring in the Carolinas was just a huge tree orgy on account of the amount of pollen they dump in the air. So, like most folks down here, we enjoy our spring drives with the windows rolled up. Thankfully, Lukus and I made a point of showerin' that mornin', so we headed on up the road smellin' sweet as flowers, without the pollen.

We diverted from Interstate 77 on over to 421 towards Boone. It didn't seem like no time before we were climbin' up the two-lane road that wound its way through Roan Mountain State Park and on up the mountain. It was then that Lukus decided to share a bit of information with me.

He sat there lookin' out the windshield, manuverin' his jeep when he casually commented, "My folks tell me there have been bears at the cabin."

He spoke so casually, I assumed he meant there had been bears seen in the woods around the mountain house. That ain't unheard of as there are black bears all over the hills dependin' on the time of year. As we pulled down the tiny one-and-a-half lane road to the cabin,

Lukus added, "When we get out, don't go out on the deck until we make sure there aren't any bears."

Now I was feelin' a mite concerned. It's one thing to have critters wanderin' around the woods. After all, that's their home, so they have the right. It's another thing for them to move in and kick back on the same deck we use to contemplate the mysteries of life.

Lukus kept on talkin'. "My folks said they cleaned up a lot of bear scat this morning, so they know the bears were up here last night. My dad said we should probably avoid the deck at night."

Now, this had me even more concerned on account of us arriving just after dark. "Do you reckon it's safe to be here tonight?"

Lukus grew up in these hills, and he's one of the calmest men I know. That's one of the reasons we're so close, but sometimes he can be a mite too lackadaisical. He smiled and told me, "Don't worry, Lucius. I doubt they're around here. If there was a problem, my dad would have told me."

I couldn't shake the thought that his daddy did tell him there was a problem. I felt really naked steppin' out of the vehicle without my rifle. If I had known there were bears around, I would have been loaded for them. We managed to get the truck unloaded without incident, and I was startin' to think I had gotten panicked over nothin'.

Of course, curiosity got the better of me, and I said we should check out the deck. After all, we could see it right outside the window, and we didn't see no bears pacing about. Lukus and I went outside to check things out and to have a look at the lights in the valley below and the heavens above. God's galaxy is quite the site to see at four thousand feet. As soon as we walked outside, we got a whiff of something powerfully foul. I felt somethin' crunch under my foot, and that was when we realized most of the deck was still covered in bear scat.

I looked over at Lukus. "I thought your folks cleaned this up."

Lukus just shook his head. "I thought they did too."

Well, Lukus being the good host he is, went right to cleanin' that mess off the deck. That smell wouldn't leave right away though. Lukus suggested we head on inside, but I needed to call Darla and tell her we had gotten there okay. For some fool reason, the cell phone coverage was sparse up on that mountainside. If you want to make a call, you have to stand out on the deck. The last thing I wanted to do was stay out there near that smell, but I knew Darla would worry if I didn't call just long enough to say we had arrived alright.

So, Lukus went on in, and I stayed out and dialed up Darla. I heard her answer and ask, "Hi, you both made it okay?"

"We did," I said. "But you won't believe what I'm smellin'. They've had bears up here on the deck, and there was scat everywhere. Lukus cleaned it up, but I'm still smellin' it."

"Do you need to go?" Darla asked.

I was in a mood to talk a few minutes. "No, I can deal with it. I'll just walk around and see if I can find a spot that don't stink so bad."

So, I walked around while Darla and I chatted. That was when I noticed somethin' peculiar. I started describing it to Darla on the phone. "You know, when I stand near the door or the steps it ain't half bad, but when I go to this far corner it stinks somethin' powerful. Lawd, woman, you wouldn't believe the smell."

Darla responded with her normal insight, "Well, silly, don't stand there."

She was right of course, but my curiosity had a hold of me. I leaned over the railing, and son of a gun, the smell about knocked me off my feet. I ain't never smelled nothin' so awful. It was like Wobbly had gone out and rolled around in somethin' dead. Even stranger, it seemed to rise up in short quick waves of nastiness. Unfortunately, I was night blind on account of the lights shining through the large windows behind me. I put my hands on the post and leaned way over to see what was stinkin'

That was the moment I knew I wasn't alone. I heard what sounded like a grunt, a sort of scraping noise, a loud thud on the ground directly below, and then somethin' heavy scufflin' through the dark followed by brush getting' knocked out of the way. The smell had disappeared, but that didn't matter much then because I had a fair idea of what had just happened.

I heard Darla's voice on the end of the phone, "You alright? What's going on?"

I started lookin' around, half expectin' to see a bear walkin' up the stairs from below. I decided it was time to say goodbye, and I told Darla, "I'm fine. I think I was just standing over top of bear hangin' on to the deck post."

"You need to hang up and go inside."

I decided I wouldn't take the time to argue that I wasn't that thick. I simply said, "Yep, love you. Goodbye." I hung up my cell phone, darted inside the back door, and locked the knob and deadbolt.

I was still facin' the door when I heard Lukus let out a sarcastic laugh. "Are you afraid someone is coming to get us?"

"Somethin' is more like it. There's a bear out there."

Lukus got real quiet as I walked the five steps over to the tree-limb couch. Lukus walked to the windows and started pacin' back and forth in front of them. "Are you sure it was a bear?"

I nodded. "You remember that smell when we went outside? I was standin' right over that varmint when I was speakin' to Darla. You can't imagine how powerful his foul odor is until you have him breathin' your way. I heard him shimmy down that post on the corner, and he lit off into the woods."

Lukus stood there for a moment, and then he sat down at the kitchen table next to the window. "You're sure?"

I nodded again. "I just hope these windows are strong if he does come back and decides to try and come inside. After all, it's the drought that has them coming to the cabins. If he gets a whiff of my honey moonshine, he's liable to break right through one of those big ole windows."

Lukus gave his usual lackadaisical shrug. "We should be fine."

I offered up some good advice, "Well, if we cook, we should do it in the daytime, and otherwise go to town to eat. I've been campin' in bear country. If you leave food out, they will come on up to where people are if they are hungry enough."

"Yea, I suppose you just proved that. Alright, but I was wanting beer chili while we are up here."

Lukus can make some mighty good beer chili. Bears or no bears, we were going to have some of that chili goodness.

"Well," I said, "I suppose your chili is worth the risk. Let's just agree to get up early to start cookin' it so we can have it before sundown. If them bears get a whiff of it, they'll be sneakin' up on us and breakin' through those windows for sure."

I didn't get much sleep. Every bump and groan around that cabin kept me awake. I was sure a ragin' black bear was goin' to burst through the window, his hide bleedin' with chunks of glass stuck into him. Then he'd see me layin' on the couch and use me as a buffet right before he found my moonshine and laid on the floor enjoyin' that mason jar's effects.

I had never been so happy to see sunrise. There were no bears around, but as the rising sun started to light up the sky, I noticed fresh bear scat since our cleanup from the night before. I cracked open the door out to the deck. Although the scat was prevalent, it didn't smell near as foul as the odors from the night before. I reckoned that ole bear decided the glass was worth leavin' in place. At least I was feelin' safer inside again.

While the nocturnal wildlife went back to sleep, I stood out there and looked over yonder at the mountains, valleys, and sky. Even with my jacket on, the cool, brisk air sent a shock through my system. It was almost as powerful as the coffee I had brewing inside. I stood there in the silence, amazed that this spot that had brought personal danger just a few hours ago now brought me only peace. I suppose that's the miracle of God's creation. Both its terrors and peace remind us we are mortal and should appreciate every sunrise while we are able.

My epiphany of life was interrupted by the realization that I was gettin' chilled down to my bones, and I didn't have any coffee to warm myself up. I wandered on back inside the house and grabbed me a freshly brewed cup from the coffeemaker. I don't know what it is, but coffee always tastes better when you realize you ain't got nothin' important to do for the day.

Well, at least I thought I was not goin' to be doin' anythin' important as the sun felt warmer comin' through the glass against my body with the woodstove glowin' behind me. It always seems like the slowest days end up the most excitin' at some point.

Lukus finally rolled his lazy tail out of bed. He announced he had forgotten the beer for the chili. Inside I was fit to be tied, but outside I just smiled and told Lukus we could go pick us up some as soon as he was ready to go.

We headed off around ten in the morning in search of some beer for the chili. Now Lukus normally uses cheap beer, and the cheaper the better. I suppose that makes sense on account of it cookin' on down into the meat and beans. However, I've always been a big believer in the idea that you should avoid cookin' with somethin' you would not partake in on its own. So, instead of goin' to the corner grocery and getting' what was on sale, I insisted we try and find us some beer from a microbrewery. That way, we could drink what we didn't cook.

Now, the northeast Tennessee hills ain't known for their beer, although they could give me pretty fair competition on my moonshine. To make Lukus happy, we did stop at the corner grocery at the bottom of the mountain. Just as I figured, there was not a single beer that I would even let Wobbly drink. So, we started on down the road. Lukus groused at me on account of the effort we were puttin' into a single bottle of beer for his chili, but I assured him we were bound to find somethin' between the cabin and the next town. After all, I wasn't that picky, but I did want somethin' that didn't taste the same going in as it likely did comin' out.

Not long after I gave Lukus my reassurance, we saw this blueish-gray building with large letterin' that read, *Beer Wash*. I pointed and said emphatically, "There we go. Pull in."

Lukus nodded and whipped his jeep into the parkin' lot. I noticed a couple of cars and motorcycles parked along the side. This must be a good place given it was in a relatively remote location and it still had customers. I hopped on out of the car and urged Lukus to hurry up.

I opened the door and let Lukus go first. I took one step inside and immediately knew this was not the sort of place I was expectin'. A group of motorcycle enthusiasts sat at a round table near a television. They were dressed in black leather pants, leather vests, and had chains linking their wallets and belt loop—and that was the women. The men wore much the same outfit, except their biceps were twice as large as the women in the group and a fair size larger than my own.

I look wide-eyed around the joint. I was all confused. It looked like a bar, except there were beers inside wall-mounted refrigerators like you might see at the local Kroger. There was a fella behind a bar that had nothing but beers chillin' on shelves behind him. I looked at Lukus, and he looked as confused as I felt.

About that time, one of the bikers spoke up and asked, "What do you boys need?"

I wanted to say I needed to get the heck out of there, but I did not want to risk insultin' anyone in their group. I started stammerin', "We need a beer. Just one beer. We're makin' some chili."

I reckon I sounded pretty ridiculous, and the group of motorcycle enthusiasts started laughin'. Of course, by that point, I was in a full panic. I wondered if any of those large gentlemen could outrun me in their tight leather pants and was afraid of what might happen if they could. However, I couldn't stay any longer as I knew we didn't belong in that establishment.

I looked at Lukus and said, "I don't see what we're lookin' for. I think we should probably go."

Lukus did not seem to pick up on the vibe in the room and responded, "There's a lot of beer here. Let's just pick one."

The bartender said, "You need to buy more than one beer." The look on Lukus's face said all I needed to know. He looked back at our motorcycle friends laughing and the bartender smirking.

He finally turned to me and said, "Yea, I think you're right."

We both raised up our hands and said, "Sorry," as we backed out of the Beer Wash. As soon as our butts had cleared the doors, we made a beeline for that jeep and prayed it would start on the first crank.

As I made my way quickly into the passenger seat, I happened to look down at my shirt. Darla had given me what I used to call, God shirts. They had a short message from God on them that was humorous and designed to make you think about the Almighty. Looking down, I saw my shirt read, *I saw what you did…God*. I shook my head as I started mumbling about how foolish I'd been and how lucky we were to get out of there in one piece.

Lukus looked over at me and asked, "What is your problem?"

I just kept shaking my head. "What are you doin'? Get us out of here before somebody decides to come and see if we left."

He cranked up that jeep and got us out on the road.

"Okay, what's up?" asked Lukus.

I realized Lukus would not leave me alone, so I told him to glance at my shirt. The jeep started a jerkin' and weavin' down the road as Lukus laughed. I hollered that he needed to get himself under control, and then I bust out laughin' too.

I finally got a hold of myself and said, "I reckon I know what those bikers were laughin' at."

Lukus got a serious look on his face. "I don't think that's what they were laughing at. That shirt might have saved us. They probably took us for a couple choir boys."

Lukus's words rang true, and I got real serious and took a long breath. "Lukus, let's not go to the Beer Wash again."

Lukus smiled and nodded in agreement. We both decided at that point it was probably best to just drive on into town and try one of the larger grocery store chains in the area. Of course, up in the mountains, most towns only have one large grocery store, not counting the local Walmart. It only took us about twenty minutes to get there. Lukus and I made a beeline for the beer section. The long refrigerated row was covered with beer as far as I could see.

Unfortunately, most of the beers were wrapped up in the typical aluminum that adds to the flavor of the pale, yellow, watered down beverages. I was beginning to think that we should have bought us a six-pack from the friendly bikers back at the Beer Wash when my eyes spied the amber bottles and familiar label of Sam Adams. I grabbed a six-pack before somebody leaked out they had real beer in town, and Lukus and I headed to the cash register.

On the way, we passed by a local who took a moment to glance at the cardboard container of beer bottles I cradled like a mother holds her child. He looked up and me with a smirk. "Import, huh?"

I started to reply, but then my brain kicked in before I could speak. The little voice inside my head reminded me that not everyone understands that Southern states are part of the US, especially when you get into some of the more remote areas. I reckoned news just ain't reached them after 150 years. So, I assumed that was why this misinformed gentleman did not recognize the name of one of our founding fathers. I thought about helping this fella out with his history, but it was getting late, and we still had not started our chili.

I just looked back at the stranger as he picked up his six-pack of Miller Lite cans and said, "Yep."

Lukus and I made our way to the cash register, trying not to snicker, which only made things worse for us. By the time we crawled into his jeep, we were cackling like his daughter and her friends when they talk about the local boy who ran his bicycle into a parked car while smilin' at them on their way to school. I calmed down, reminded Lukus of our quest for some food, and he nodded as he got us back on up to the cabin.

By the time we got back up to our house on the side of the mountain, there was even more bear scat on the deck. We both agreed we would simply admire the view from indoors the remainder of the trip. Lukus started makin' us chili, and I opened up a couple of the extra bottles of imported beer for the two of us.

It didn't take much time for the smell of Lukus's famous beer chili to fill that cabin. At that point, both Lukus and I turned and faced the windows. We were both concerned about where that bear was and if he could smell our delicious late afternoon meal. I wandered on downstairs a couple of times, worried about what I might find on the bottom deck.

Thankfully, that old bear never did show up again. That didn't stop Lukus and me from standin' sentinel around the place for the rest of the weekend. I personally was happy to see the weekend end for once. I am a big believer in relaxin' when I take time off from work. I think the next time I head up that way I'll take my trusty shotgun and some rock salt. I doubt I will ever use it, but it makes me feel safe, like a teddy bear.

BATTERED BY
HURRICANE FLOYD

I have me all sorts of friends from all over God's good earth. Despite what some folks think, not everybody in the South is a hillbilly or redneck. One of my good friends is a Yankee from up in New England. His name is Jeff. Ole Jeff and I worked together for a lot of years back in my computer days. He had himself a mess of children, just like Darla and me. So, anytime we could take a family vacation together, we jumped at the opportunity. After all, youngin' tend to entertain themselves when they are around each other, sort of like short adults.

Jeff had a buddy who owned a beach house out yonder on Oak Island. He offered up his place to both our families, and Jeff and I knew we had to take advantage of this golden opportunity. Another thing our families had in common was homeschoolin'. Because we taught our kids on our schedule, it allowed us to take our vacations anytime we liked. Jeff's buddy offered us his place for September. This is when everybody else's family is back to school and work here in the Carolinas, so we knew we had the beach practically to ourselves.

Fortunately, early fall in the Carolinas still feels a lot like summer, so when we arrived at the beach, the sun, sand, and water wrapped around all of us like a warm hug from a friend. We let the youngin's go crazy in the water while we adults lay out on the beach pretending to watch everything them rug rats was doin'. To tell the truth, we did have some mighty young children back in those days, and Darla and Jeff's wife, Lucy, did keep a hawk's eye on the smallest of 'em.

We really didn't spend much time in the house, except for meals and sleepin'. With such a mess of children, eatin' out was hard to do. One meal would have cost us more money than that entire trip put together. Fortunately, we had a kitchen system. The older kids would help get the meal ready, and our wives supervised 'em. We husbands helped out by watchin' the television and tellin' the younger children to keep the noise down and not to kill each other.

The house we stayed in was your typical beach house. The layout had more bedrooms than anybody would ever need for themselves. That's because beach homeowners know they'll always have company. This house was special though, on account of the way it was built for hurricanes. If you don't know already, hurricanes are given a scale, or category, based on wind speeds and what have you. Most houses in the Carolinas are built for a category two hurricane. That's a pretty normal storm since the state sits between the really warm waters of the Gulf and southern Atlantic, and the cooler water of the Yankees.

The owner of this house had gone a step above and built it to withstand a category four hurricane. That meant he wouldn't see any real damage until the winds reached at least 130 miles per hour. I have to admit, the only thing I've ever seen built that sturdy was my barn, but the beach house looked a whole lot different than my outbuildin'.

To begin with, it was built on stilts, or I should say steel poles that were painted white to blend in with the neighbors' wooden sticks that held up their houses. As an added measure, the owner had put a huge steel beam down the center of the elevated floor to hold that house in place. On the outside, he had screwed in every yellow board attached to that house. He had even screwed in the shingles on the roof. The interior had a tongue and groove pine ceilin'. Those were screwed in, and of course, all the drywall was all screwed in. That was the most screwed house I have ever seen.

Even with all the youngin's hollerin', screamin', playin', and stompin', the house stayed relatively quiet. We didn't hear a lot of noise from the other rooms. I reckon this was on account of all them screws. Those first couple of days were heaven for both the kids and the adults. On the third day, I decided to bring up The Weather Channel on the television on account of no sports bein' broadcast. We make it a rule to shy away from news on vacation, but we were plannin' on takin' a trip to one of the outer banks while we were there, so the weather news became a priority.

That was when we first heard about the powerful storm headin' our way. Hurricane Floyd was due to hit the coast in the next forty-eight hours. The good news was that it was supposed to make landfall around Charleston and then head on up the same path as Hugo. That meant the hurricane would miss us, unless of course, we went home early. Even my Yankee friend could see how stayin' at the beach was better than headin' home to face the winds of a hurricane or tropical storm.

There was another plus to stayin' at the beach. The waves got mighty big, which meant we would have us some fine boogie boardin' conditions. Of course, that brought its own issues. Here in the Carolinas our coast is made up of a lot of sand. Now, that can be fun if you want to go scuba divin' or just walk out several yards off the coast. Then again, if you get an itch to head out too far you're liable to run into some shark swimmin' up and down the coastline. They aren't bad fish, but a body can get awful hungry swimmin' all the time, and you could find yourself becomin' an afternoon snack for the critter.

Assumin' you don't mind a few sharks, there is one other problem along the beautiful beaches of the Carolinas. Riptides. Now if you ain't never been caught up in one, it can be a pretty enlightin' experience. When the waves get big, they get to shiftin' all that sand around, and pretty soon a trough gets formed. Well, sir, between that trough and all the gyrations of the water, you can find yourself pulled further out into the ocean than you had planned. Unfortunately, unless you know better, you're liable to wind up fish food, or blue, swollen, and layin' on the beach without any air left in your body. That sort of thing can ruin a good vacation.

Now, the only way to break free from a riptide is to swim sideways, and I don't mean swimmin' side to side. You have to swim parallel to the coastline. It sounds really easy, but it don't make a lot of sense when you are swimming along the coastline and still gettin' pulled out into the ocean. However, you'll eventually break free of the water's hidden river. Then you just point your body towards shore and take your time gettin' back to the warm, dry sand. Normally, if the waves are decent, the last few yards can be accomplished by allowin' your body fat to float you on in with the waves.

Needless to say, when the swells are worth gettin' out on with a boogie board or surfboard, they can be considerably dangerous, and so you should respect them. This is why I made sure the children had their boogie board leashes secured around their ankles when we hit the beaches as the waves got bigger from the distant hurricane.

Most days the waves on that beach were three feet tall when they were feeling ambitious, but this day they were runnin' between six and ten feet. I knew it was not only a good opportunity for me to get some boogie boardin' in, but it was a good chance for my eight and ten-year-old boys to gain some valuable experience. Fortunately, the riptides hadn't had a chance to get too strong yet, but there was one other small problem.

In North Carolina, they let folks build houses right up along the beaches. I guess they ain't never read the Bible where Jesus talks about the fool that builds his house on the sand. Predictably, when the storms do come, most of those houses end up floatin' on out into the water. This is why readin' is important. If folks read their Bible, they'd know better than to build their house on the beach. Of course, a lot of those same people go back and build another house on the same spot, so maybe it ain't ignorance, just stupidity.

Because folks insist on buildin' on the sand, the beach can become a pretty crowded place when the waves get high. So, as we were out there slippin' down the rollin' hills of water, we started gettin' pushed closer and closer to those beach houses. Before long, we found ourselves sort of bobbin' and weavin' between pillars of folks' decks. So, I did what any responsible parent would do. I told the kids to be sure and aim between the houses when they got pushed on into shore.

We had us a big ole time in the water. Some of the full-timers who actually live in the town came on out to look at the waves and sort of stared at us out in the water with the kids. I guess the fact that we were the only ones in the water at the time had somethin' to do with their curiosity. I couldn't understand how anyone could let those waves pass on by without gettin' their boards wet.

Everything was goin' according to plan. The kids were stayin' where it was shallow and gettin' in some fun rides. None of us had managed to hit any parts of a house yet, and the larger fish seemed to be stayin' away for some reason. That was when things began to take a turn. I saw a wave comin' in that was about eight feet tall. My ten-year-old decided he was goin' to take a shot at ridin' it. I was there tryin' to coach him to step a few feet out further and then hop on the board. I guess the only thing that youngin' heard was to hop on the board. I realized too late that young man had placed himself right in the path of where the wave would come crashin' down. I yelled for him to hold his breath when that water landed on top of him.

He disappeared from view, and I desperately looked around for him. I started workin' my way towards shore and was relieved to see him rollin' up on the wet sand spittin' out seawater. I couldn't help myself and stood there laughin' while the waves were bouncin' up against me. The poor child decided he had enough, and I can't say as I blamed him. So, he went up and sat down to watch us, like all the sensible folks were doing.

I swam back out and caught me a nice ten-foot wave. As I finished out the ride on the whitewater, I noticed a septic tank exposed in the sand near a house, and that was when I started to thinkin' that maybe we should be gettin' out of the water. When I hollered at Darla and the others that we should probably call it a day, I notice my eight-year-old driftin' out. Evidently, he had got on his board waitin' on a wave that never came. Instead, he managed to catch a mild riptide.

I put my board up on the sand and swam back out into the water to his board. We spent some quality time talkin' about the value of listenin' to your elders as I pulled us out of the small current and then back towards the shore. We both enjoyed the ride back in once we caught back up to the waves. Fortunately for me, I have enough body fat that a boogie board is really an optional device. The wives and kids were in, and we headed back to the beach house across the road feelin' tired and pleased with our events of the afternoon.

Before long, the women were cookin' supper, and us men were supervisin' the television and the kids again while we checked on the hurricane. The weatherman said that Floyd was still headin' towards Charleston, and the outer bands would hit Oak Island, but it wouldn't be too serious. We parents segregated ourselves away from the youngin's durin' dinner so we could figure out some activities for the next day given we'd probably be stuck inside with the rain for at least part of the day.

We finally got all the kids to bed by ten o'clock, and the four of us rested and enjoyed the peaceful house. Unfortunately, outside it was not near as peaceful. The wind was pickin' up, lightnin' crackled, and thunder rolled. My buddy Jeff and I decided to check out The Weather Channel for more information on Floyd. We left the sound off to make sure we didn't wake up any of our rug rats. Lookin' at the radar, we could see the top part of the storm hittin' the island. That explained the racket outside. However, the worst of the storm still appeared aimed at our houses back in Charlotte. We all discussed it and still agreed it was smartest to stay put and enjoy the beach before we had to head home and deal with the mess that would be waitin' for us.

After all the lights were out, Darla and I opened the blinds and enjoyed the light show God had goin' on in the sky. It ain't every night the sky lights up brighter than a Krispy Kreme neon sign. The thunder rolled so continuously it sounded as though it penetrated the walls and rumbled right on through the house. It was very excitin', but the day's activities had left us exhausted, and before long, we were fast asleep.

The next mornin', I woke up before the rest of the house. I wanted to enjoy a little more peace and quiet before the gaggle of children and adults awoke to discover the dark clouds and rain that would surely leave us housebound for most of our day. The rain beat hard against the house, and the wind was now howlin'. I looked out the front window that faced the road and the beach beyond. Imagine my surprise when I saw the waves crashin' against the road and seawater flowin' beneath our cars and the house.

I had a feelin' the weatherman may have been a bit mistaken in his forecast. I clicked on the television and turned up the sound to hear it over the dronin' of the rain. I knew that would alert the house, but at this point, I was thinkin' that wasn't such a bad idea. Much to my surprise, I saw the hurricane had skirted on up the coast, and the eye was creepin' right towards us. Feelin' a mite panicked, I rushed back to the window. A large, red fire truck with its lights on slowly cruised down the wave-crested road. I cracked open the front door to hear a fireman speakin' into the loudspeaker tellin' whoever was stupid enough to still be there to evacuate immediately.

About that time, the house was wakin' up on account of the television, I started to get uptight because I noticed the water comin' across the road was a couple inches deeper than it was just thirty minutes before. It brought to mind my old pickup that I got into a pool of saltwater on the coast after a hurricane. It did all sorts of damage to my poor engine. I did not have the time, or money, to let that happen to the family minivan. Worse, I had images of it bein' carried out by the waves as we all sat stranded on our stilted island with the ocean ebbing to and fro beneath.

I let Jeff know that it was time to head back to Charlotte, but he started insistin' that we should clean the beach house before we evacuate. We began arguin' back and forth about the value of cleaning a house that may not be standin' in a few hours, especially if we were inside it when it fell to the ground. It didn't matter what I said, Jeff was determined to clean that house. After all, there were twelve of us stayin' in it and only four of us were adults. I finally capitulated because Jeff was a Yankee, and no self-respectin' Southerner was goin' to let their hospitality be outdone by a Yankee.

So, we lined up the kids, assigned each one to a cleanin' task while we adults start runnin' through our respective mental checklist to make sure we weren't forgetting to pack nothin'. Jeff and I headed out to start packin' our vehicles. Now, I ain't never had rain hit me at over eighty miles per hour. I learned right quick that those watery pellets hurt right much when they smacked you in the face at that speed.

Jeff and I were hangin' onto our minivans, lookin' like somethin' from an old silent movie comedy. Wind blew my soft roof pod this way and that. Everything was soaked, and I felt like an idiot tryin' to protect my wet belongin's from the weather by putting them in my wet roof pod. However, when you have a big family, space inside the vehicle is a premium, so I pressed on. Jeff and I finally managed to throw our stuff in on top or inside the cars and went rushin' up the stairs and back inside the dry house.

I reckoned the storm must have been pickin' up on us while we were packin' because that wind and rain were makin' an awful racket against the beach house now. The kids were quiet as they focused on gettin' their chores done. I was still grousin' with my friend about the wisdom of our decision when the house phone rang. Jeff picked it up, and it was his friend that owned the place.

He asked what we thought we were doin' still bein' there, and Jeff explained we are sprucin' up the place before we headed out. I didn't hear his buddy's response, but I reckoned he gave Jeff a piece of his mind. Jeff hung up the phone and announced we were all leavin' immediately per the instructions of the home's owner.

Up until this point, nobody but Jeff and me had thought about what it would be like to exit the well-built walls, but when we opened that front door, everybody got an education. Rain pelted the kids' faces, and they fussed and hollered as they headed for the minivans. Darla had our youngest wrapped in her coat tryin' to protect him. Fortunately, we had one of the newfangled minivans with two side-doors, so we had the kids pile in on the side the wind wasn't drivin' the rain against. I looked down as I was shovin' kids into the safety of the vehicle and notice the ocean was washin' over the top of my feet.

We got the last one in, and I hollered for everyone to buckle up. Darla didn't need any motivation to climb into the passenger seat, and I put my head down and let the rain batter against my bald head as I pushed my way around to the driver's side. We volunteered to take one of Jeff's kids on account of him throwin' more supplies inside the vehicle than on the roof. This meant he was able to load up quicker, and he was already backin' out by the time my wet butt hit the driver's seat, but we were right on his bumper in a matter of seconds.

It was a surreal feelin' to see the ocean's waves crashin' on one side of the road and flowin' across underneath the minivans. Jeff made a quick left at the first road to get away from the waves. Unfortunately, we were on an island. Of course, in the Carolinas words like *island* or *isle* is fancy talk for *sandbar*. Rememberin' my history, I recalled how Cape Hatteras and other "islands" had been cut in half by hurricanes, and I began to think that we should expedite our evacuation.

My next thought was to the bridge we were drivin' towards. I hadn't seen any emergency vehicles since we left the house, which meant they had all left the island, and I was beginin' to worry that the bridge might be closed. I prayed awful hard to the Almighty as we approached the overpass for the now flooded Intracoastal Waterway. Seein' the bridge open, we slowly made away across as the wind howled around our vehicles. Once we were safely on the mainland, we eased our way through town until we hit the two-lane highway headin' west.

I had my bumper practically kissin' Jeff's car on account of him goin' the speed limit. I looked around at the low lyin' sand marshes that surround the road, and I commented to Darla that we were goin' to get washed off the road if we spent too much time in the area. Given the flatlands lasted fifty miles or so, I knew we should think about expeditin' our evacuation. I decided to turn on the local radio to listen for flood warnin's. To my surprise, there wasn't any talk of flash floodin'. I think this was on account of the emergency broadcast system squawkin' through the car speakers every few minutes to announce a new tornado in our vicinity.

I had been blown off the highway by the leadin' edge of a tornado before, and it was not somethin' I wanted to repeat. I was all over Jeff's rear end at this point, hopin' he would catch the hint. Out of frustration, I asked Darla to call them. She rang his wife's cell phone and was explainin' that we need to get on out of the area.

Darla looked over at me and said that Jeff thought we'd be okay. It was at that moment that I realized a powerful truth about Yankees. When it comes to the wintertime and snow, there are few folks that know more about drivin' in the snow on the East Coast than a New Englander. However, when it comes to hurricanes, those poor masses ain't got no more clue than a blind man drivin' off the side of a bridge.

I realized at that point that Jeff only had one oar in the water and was makin' the wrong decision. Jeff's kid was in my vehicle, so I hated to take off and leave his family in my rearview mirror. On the other side of that equation were tornados, floods, and of course, the eye of the storm directly behind us.

I realize some folks readin' this may be thinkin', "What about the wind or hydroplaning off the road?" I reckon I should pause a moment and share that Darla and I knew these roads better than our own children.

Back when we attended college and were datin', Darla and I used to drive these roads to and from campus with our friends. In those days, we had old vehicles that had what was called "play" in the steering. That meant you could turn the steerin' wheel a half inch or so in either direction before the wheels began to turn. We would take our cars down these roads at seventy and eighty miles per hour. Of course, bein' in college, we were convinced we were immortal, so we weren't concerned with gettin' hurt.

Since we were indestructible, and things like cell phones had not been invented, we would pass notes between the cars via our windows as we went cruisin' down the highway. So, drivin' in a twenty-first-century minivan with its high-end suspension, onboard computer, and high-end traction tires was a cakewalk, even in the most inclement of weather. I looked over at Darla and told her if Jeff's wife called to tell them we'd meet them back at the house.

I felt a smile creep across my lips as I took the oncoming lane, pressed down on the accelerator, and blew past my friend. There was not a soul on that flat, straight two-lane road but us. I knew the police weren't around since they had to deal with the storm. In fact, if it hadn't been for the good Lord lettin' that storm head our way, I believe I could have had that minivan pushin' a hundred easy. Once I got her past seventy miles per hour, I started noticin' the wind pushin' hard against the car. On the plus side, the higher speed helped shed the rain off the windshield.

As the minivan and I began to settle into our rhythm, Darla's phone went off. I looked in my rearview mirror, and Jeff's vehicle was not much more than a speck, but I noticed he wasn't gettin' any smaller either. Darla looked over at me, and I have to admit, I had a broad smile that I wasn't shy about hidin' from my bride. She grinned back and answered the phone.

Sure enough, Jeff's wife was sayin' Jeff was a fussin' about my speed and that I needed to remember his kid was in my car. I hollered over and asked if they had been listenin' to the weather alerts. Darla relayed the question, took the phone away from her ear, and shook her head as she explained that they had been listening to CDs. I started mumblin' some unkind words below the drone of the engine and rain.

I reckon they must of turned on the radio around that point because Darla hung up the phone and said Jeff promised to try and keep up.

We went barrelin' down that highway. Wind buffeted that minivan one direction, and then another, and then not at all. Rain pounded different sides of the car and the front windshield. We practically had to yell to hear each other. Above this racket, I had the radio blarin' so I could hear if we were headin' into some new tornado we had yet to hear about or if there was a flash flood up ahead. Needless to say, we weren't bored.

An hour into the drive, I noticed the wind was startin' to slow down, and twenty minutes later, the rain stopped, and I could see sunshine. It only just began to dawn on me that the radio was now playin' music instead of emergency broadcast. I brought my speed down to just ten over the speed limit. The local weather came on to tell us that Floyd was starting to make its turn north and was expected to just clip the Charlotte area. We were still an hour and a half from home, so I knew we weren't out of the woods yet.

At that point, we started hittin' some of the larger towns as we got further west into the state. The highway changed to four lanes and then to town roads, followed by highway off and on. As we drove into Laurenburg, I noticed the traffic lights were all set to blinkin' yellow to ensure folks could escape the hurricane.

By then we were baskin' in the warm sun and blue sky. I turned on the car's air conditioner on account of the humid eighty plus degrees of a mid-fall Southern day. If it wasn't for the dark skies to the east, we would have completely forgotten about our previous brush with a windy and watery oblivion. Given the miles we still had to drive to get home, I pulled the car in to get gas, and Jeff joined us a couple of minutes later.

I explained to Jeff that we shouldn't rest on our laurels because the storm was still chasin' us, and we should get home before the leading edge caught up. This time Jeff was of a mind to listen to me. We hit the road and cruised on down the highway. I finally let myself relax and commented on the fact that all the empty roads were makin' for a downright pleasant return home. At least they were until I suddenly had to hit my brakes. Before me sat two lines of cars for as far as the eye could see. Evidently, we had caught up with the rest of the stupid people who had not evacuated when they should have.

It felt downright surreal. One minute we were driving home on empty roads with the hurricane slowly sinkin' from view, and now we were stopped in a long line of cars along an empty section of highway. When we did mosey along, it wasn't for very long. At first, I thought there must have been a bad wreck, but I saw no cars comin' east, and so I was really confused. It was possible some terrible tragedy had occurred to close down the entire highway, but I was gettin' nothin' on the radio.

For two hours, we crept along that asphalt. I was thankful I had filled up our gas tank, or by this point, we might have been stranded on the side of the road. We were on the edge of a town called Hamlet when I notice the sun disappear. Suddenly, the radio squawked its first emergency broadcast about the oncomin' storm. We had been stuck in traffic for so long that Floyd had caught up to us.

The rain and wind started to pick up. I looked around us and notice how the road rose and dipped with the landscape. I should say it was more like the road was flat, with occasional low spots. I knew we were in a flash flood zone, but there was nothin' I could do now since there weren't any open lanes to take advantage of. I could only pray, creep the car along, and hope we could get out of the area in time.

We got into downtown Hamlet, North Carolina about an hour later. By that point, the rain was once again comin' down in sheets, and the wind was pushin' against the side of our vehicle. As we approached the center of town, I saw the source of our trouble. The local leaders had decided that the hurricane did not warrant a change in their traffic patterns to handle the evacuation. So, our four-lane highway dropped to a two-lane road through the middle of town, complete with a four-way traffic light that had stopped thousands of evacuating cars dead in their tracks.

By the time we got to the light and turned right to continue on through the rest of town, the roads were startin' to hold the water that'd been rainin' down on them. Traffic suddenly stopped in front of me, and I hit my brakes. The brakes took a second or two to rub off the water and catch. That had me squirmin' like a worm in hot ashes since I had been ridin' my brakes most of the way through town. We finally got to the edge of town, and traffic was sparse. Everyone was hittin' the gas and loaded for bear. By this point, Jeff and I were in a practical race back home. Every town after Hamlet had their lights fixed and lanes open for the business of evacuation. We made record time back to the homestead near Charlotte.

Unfortunately, Floyd had managed to get so far past us that it was rainin' at the house. We helped Jeff reorganize his vehicle so all his kids could fit. Although we were gettin' wet, at least the rain didn't feel like BBs hittin' our faces. He left for his house, and I got busy unloadin' the car. Darla told me I should wait for the rain to let up, but I was worried about the wet luggage in the wet roof pod. Somewhere inside my pea pickin' mind I was afraid the supplies might get wetter. By the time I finished unloadin', I was soaked to the gills.

A mess of baths and showers later, we settled in for the evenin'. The phone rang just as things settled down, and it was Jeff. He informed me that his house was sunny. Evidently, twenty miles west where his family lived was just outside the storm's edge. I thanked him for the information and a memorable vacation before hangin' up and mumblin' to myself about Yankees. The rain outside my home was fallin' steady as I turned on the news.

The local folks let us know we would get several inches of much-needed rain for our area before the storm completed its northern turn on up to New England where they could expect large amounts of rainfall. I smiled and nodded as the station went to commercial. When it returned, I saw footage of cars linin' Interstate 74 and the name *Hamlet* came across the bottom of the screen. I laughed and told Darla to look for our car.

Several cars were under water along the piece of highway we had left just a couple of hours previously, and they showed the local high school gym packed in with weary, and angry, travelers. It turned out I was right about that roadway. It started to flood, and the town had to go out and rescue drivers then put them in the local high school. I reckon it never occurred to them just to change that stupid intersection. Instead, they shut down the entire highway. That whole drama played out less than thirty minutes after we left the town.

I was thankin' Jesus for the time we made from our peril along the beach. As the days past, we saw photos of a familiar pink house that had sat across from the one we stayed in. Parts of it were all over what was left of the beach. Jeff's friend's house had weathered Floyd just fine. Lookin' back, I'm sure we would have been fine if we had stayed put, but our cars surely would have floated away.

The state's politicians dealt with the fallout from the Hamlet fiasco for months. Year over year, the good people of western North Carolina had requested a bypass around small towns since there was no direct highway access from the state's largest city to the coast. The bills to build one had always been tabled. This happened, in part, due to lobbying from impacted towns like Hamlet. They did not want to lose the tourist dollars that flowed in from vacationers headin' to the beach. The fallout from Hamlet's decision to shut down the road was the tippin' point. In a few short months, money was allocated and contracts awarded.

Although it's not totally complete, the majority of the highway now runs to the coast and bypasses a majority of the towns. Hamlet is a forgotten memory on an exit sign along the speedy bypass. Thanks to the efforts of its local leaders, they have maintained their town's two lanes through the middle of the sleepy village, and their community will no longer need to worry about havin' to house evacuees stranded by their lack of infrastructure and leadership. Hurricane Floyd brought a lot of destruction to North Carolina, but thanks to that storm, infrastructure was finally improved, and that has helped bring more goods and tourists down east.

Blind as a Bat

Now I ain't one who goes around yellin' about miracles or jumpin' pews. I did try a pew jumpin' church once when I was a young man. I knew it was not for me when I missed my jump, hit my shin, and face planted into the back of the next bench. As I sat there with my forehead bleedin' and a lot of well-meanin' folks prayin' on me instead of applyin' a bandage, I realized the Almighty was givin' me a message. He was lettin' me know I should sit down, shut up, and listen to what He has to say. It's a lesson I've learned pretty well over the years. Repeatedly.

I reckon the years as a young man taught me I should work hard, try and live the kind of life I claimed to follow in church, and avoid gettin' in the kind of trouble that would be embarassin' to my parents if they saw me on the evening news. I did this for a lot of years, and I came out the better for it. At least until one mornin' when the good Lord decided it was time to stir things up a bit.

I woke up like I did every mornin'. Although, if I'm honest, it was more like sneakin' awake. Darla is not a morning person, unless your mornin' starts after ten o'clock. So, I had a pattern of openin' my eyes to let them adjust to the risin' sun and then slidin' out of the covers. On this particular mornin', things were a bit different. My left eye seemed to be fuzzy. I worked on cleanin' out anything the sandman had left behind, but try as I might, I could not get the fuzzy vision to change. It was downright aggravatin' as it felt like someone had their hand over my eye at times.

Of course, bein' a young man, I did what all men do at that age. I slid on out of bed and went into work, ignorin' the aggravatin' vision. I didn't say anythin' to my coworkers on account of me bein' afraid that Darla might hear about it. I just assumed my eyes were tired, and

I promised myself I'd slow down on my work hours a bit until the problem passed. The next couple of days started like the first one. I woke up to find everything as blurry as I had left it the night before. This went on for about a week, but then I woke up one mornin' and everythin' changed.

My left eye felt weird, and the room itself seemed off for some reason. I was lookin' over yonder towards our dresser, and I closed my right eye. To my surprise, the entire dresser disappeared, and all I could see was the wall where the dresser had been. It looked like someone had covered it with a blanket that matched the wall. I looked around the bedroom and I could make various pieces of furniture, pictures, etc., disappear with a blink of an eye.

Now some fellas might think this is a blessin', especially if they don't like who they are sleepin' next to. Unfortunately, I'm not one of those fellas. So, the thought of not seein' Darla disturbed me somethin' fierce. I decided at this point that it was probably a good idea to risk wakin' up Darla. That's always a chancy proposition as she has been known to throw her arm wildly when she's awakened before she is ready to get out of bed.

She must have realized somethin' was off since I was wakin' her up. Instead of takin' a swing, she rolled over and asked me what was wrong. I was a little panicked inside. I started demonstratin' how I could make the furniture disappear by coverin' my right eye up. Of course, Darla could not see what I was talkin' about. Fortunately, she went ahead and took my word for it. I'm quite sure it was not nearly as dramatic as I felt it was. I got up and showered, and did all the things I usually do. I did notice somebody had gone and moved the walls a few inches. I quit fussin' about bumpin' my shoulder after the third collision with a doorway.

Darla took me over yonder to the doc. He put up one of those eye charts that have been around since Jesus walked the earth and had me read it. Fortunately, he had me use my bad eye first as I have a habit of memorizing things right quick. When I explained the top line was blurrin' and the rest were missin', he rushed me over quick to an ophthalmologist.

Now I have to confess that it was sort of nice to be fussed over. When we arrived at the ophthalmologist, they didn't even bother to make me fill out any paperwork. They just rushed me right in. The fifteen people in the waiting room looked downright annoyed. Rather, I guessed they did. I wasn't seein' the expressions of the folks on the left side of the room too well at that point.

Some doc who looked as young as me came walkin' in and asked me a bunch of medical questions. I tried to remember what all I went through as a kid without admittin' to anythin'. About the time he got done playin' twenty questions, my eyes were dilated, and I was right thankful for the overhead lights gettin' turned off. The next thing I knew, that old doc had a spotlight on top of his head pointed directly into my eye, and then he added a magnifying glass. I was feelin' a mite panicked because I remember what the sun did to the ants we used to point at with our magnifying glasses as kids.

I was doin' my best to climb out of that chair, and that ole doc just told me I needed to sit still so he didn't hurt me. At that point I'm wonderin' what sort of horror film I'd put myself in. The doc's solution to makin' you uncomfortable was to threaten you if you moved? I sat still, but inside I had images of my eyeballs bein' used for table tennis. Although it felt like an hour, I reckoned that doc only tried to fry my retinas for a few minutes. I was breathin' a sigh of relief when that spotlight finally stopped shinin'. Of course, now I was blind in my good eye too.

The doc just stood there for a few seconds and then asked me if I had a lazy eye. I was a little insulted because there ain't nothin' lazy about me. I told him nobody has ever accused me of havin' a lazy eye. He smiled, nodded, and then just left the room. His nurse, who was a bit more sociable, told me the doctor will be back and to please wait. Then she left me in there too.

By this point, I was debatin' just gettin' up and leavin'. Never mind I couldn't see half the room. I still had one good eye, and I know a lot of folks who function with just one eye. I had just been accosted, plumb near blinded in my good eye, and threatened not to move. I had put up with more than enough.

Just as I started to get out of that chair to try to find Darla, the door opened back up. I saw five white coats come in. I prayed they were eye doctors and not a bunch of folks comin' to drag me away to the funny farm. One by one, they came over and shined their bright lights into my eyes without sayin' a word. I began to wonder if I was losin' my mind and I was actually in a rubber room imagin' all of this. Finally, the parade of doctors ceased, and they were whisperin' in a corner. I will say they were far better at whisperin' than most folks, as I could not hear a word they were sayin'.

When they finished their powwow, everyone left except for the first doc who had seen me. He went on to tell me I had a rare eye condition called uveitis and maybe somethin' called Behcet's disease based on my answers to his questions, but they needed to do more testin' because there could be other reasons for the symptoms. He then handed me this ointment to put on my eye and told me if that didn't work they would try eye injections. I ain't no doctor, but I do remember my momma trainin' me to never stick needles in my eyes. We even used it as a threat to always tell the truth, so I was thinkin' I wanted to avoid that treatment.

The next day, I get ready for work, and the ointment seemed to be helpin' some. However, while drivin' home, I noticed things felt a bit out of kilter. Headin' down the road, I covered up my right eye and discovered all the cars around me no longer had license plates. I reckoned that was not a good thing, and so the next mornin' I was back at the doctor. Evidently, me bein' there annoyed him because his only response to the ointment not workin' was to tell me we had to do eye injections. He promised me it wouldn't hurt, but my eye would feel some pressure.

I asked, some might say begged, for an alternative. I was certainly inquisitive about any options, anything at all. The good doctor assured me there was a reason for the progression of treatment. I believe this is a medical professional's way of simply sayin' no. I submitted to the inevitable because I was told that if I did not let him poke me in the eye my sight loss would be permanent. The doctor asked me if I would like to do just one eye or two. I was surprised because I thought my other eye was healthy. That was when I was informed that it had the same disease, but I wasn't noticin' it on account of how bad my left eye was.

I am a right practical individual, so I tell the doctor he better do both because I doubt I will be returnin' the next day to experience this again. He asked if Darla had come with me, and I told him no, as she was takin' care of the youngin's. He said I might have trouble seein' afterwards, but that sounded a bit redundant to me, and so I told him to get on with it.

You may recall I mentioned the doctor said there would be some pressure. I reckon that's medical for your eye feelin' like it's going to explode and shoot gushy goo out of your eye socket. At least that was what it felt like when he was shootin' whatever it was inside my eyeball. On the bright side, I never felt that needle. Oh, and I was told not to move my eyeball while all this was goin' on or I would destroy my eyeball, so at least I had that knowledge comforting me as I attempted to embed myself into the back of the chair.

If I had to compare this experience to my vasectomy, I'd let that comical urologist cut on my tender parts repeatedly before doin' eye injections again. I reckoned by this point you all are probably squirmin' pretty good while you're readin' this, but the worst is over.

After we got done with both my eyeballs, I sort of sat there in shock. The doctor told me my eyesight should return to normal in a day or two, and if not, we'd look at our options. I just nodded and quickly moved towards the door. Unfortunately, it was at that moment that I realized I couldn't really see out of either eye, and the room was sort of spinnin'. I felt angry, confused, and downright irritated. I knew I needed Darla to come get me, youngin's and all. I walked over to the courtesy phone in the lobby on account of this bein' 1997. I tried to dial my home number, but I couldn't see the buttons on the phone.

I sort of lost my head and stormed out of the office towards my car. I started lookin' around and realized my world was now completely orange, and everything appeared to be fuzzy blocks like you'd see on an old Pong game or the first Nintendo. I was disoriented, angry, and ready for this day to be over. I noticed an orange-hued red square where I thought I left my car. After some feelin' around, I managed to unlock the door and get in the car.

I was convinced I was stranded and would be sittin' in the uptown Charlotte doctor's office well after midnight until a mugger found me. I put my head against my headrest and started prayin'. Suddenly, the spinning stopped. I lifted my head, and I got dizzy again. I put my head back on the headrest and began to look around. It was at that point I realized that the world really did look like a big video game. So, I started the car and headed towards my house. I had not memorized the route to work from the doctor's office, but I did know my way home.

I was in much better spirits when I pulled into our driveway. I still could not see anything more than colored squares, but I had made it home. I stumbled my way inside the house, and that was when I found out that those injections had evidently made my eyes swollen, orange, and generally speakin' pretty nasty to look at. I asked Darla to take me to work, and she told me I should not leave the house. She had always been good about lettin' me know when I'm not presentable.

I decided to head into work anyway. I figured if I looked that bad, they would send me back home. Darla carried me on into the office. I reckoned she had a feelin' we would be headin' back to the house and thought it best to just humor me because I was fit to be tied by everythin' that was happenin'. I should've turned around at the reception area at the office when our receptionist gave me a quick disgusted glance. It was the kind of look you get if you have a booger hangin' out of your nose that you don't know it's there. At least, that was how her orange, blocky head appeared to me. My boss saw me and started fussin' at me for showin' up. That was the day I learned there's a fine line between dedicated and stupid. Needless to say, I headed home.

Although the whole experience helped my eyes for a few days, I was back to Dr. Feel Good's office before the week was out. We did another round of injections, and the results were similar, both during the treatment and afterwards, although Darla did drive me home that time. At that point, I was finally given some alternatives by the good doctor. I could get even more injections, take a pill called prednisone, or let my eyes lose their sight. I considered options one and three a toss-up, so I went with the pill.

I was told that we needed to use an unusually high dose for an extended period of time because of this Behcet's disease they were testin' for, in addition to the uveitis. Evidently, the underlying disease was expected to kill me within five years if I didn't do somethin', and prednisone was the only drug at the time that had a proven track record within a relatively short time window. The doctor did warn me I'd gain some weight. At least that was what the team of doctors they had me bouncin' around between was claimin' by that point.

I was disappointed about the weight. I had focused on keepin' my weight down and had lost thirty pounds in the effort. I figured I could keep any new weight off if I applied myself, but then I was also warned not to work out because the effort could make my heart explode. That concerned me enough I took the doc's advice. The doctor did not stop with the explodin' heart and expanded belly though. He told me I would have mood swings. I thought that might be fun, what with me liking to laugh all the time and pull jokes on folks. Lastly, he said it would change my body. He said my face would become round and other things might happen, like all my body fat migrating to my stomach. When I asked what other things could happen, the doctor just shrugged and said they weren't sure. It seemed they had never put a patient on 120 milligrams of the stuff for several weeks before. I left with a list of side effects and a drug that would hopefully help me see.

Lawd, that doctor was not kiddin' about them side effects. That first week I gained back all thirty pounds, and that wasn't even from eatin'. I just sort of ballooned up. My clothes were too tight, and my face looked like it belonged on somebody else's shoulders. To make matters worse, if I avoided eatin', I would get the shakes like my meth-addicted cousin Ed. I was only sleepin' three hours a night on account of my brain wantin' to work all the time. After a couple of days, I gave up and started goin' into work at five o'clock in the mornin' just to have somethin' to do. Most days I kept workin' until seven at night just to avoid drivin' Darla and the kids crazy. At least my vision had come back, and that was a good thing.

The doctor was able to slowly get the dose to eighty milligrams after about three weeks, and I was up to two-hundred-and-sixty pounds from one-hundred-and-sixty-five. No matter what I tried, the weight refused to drop off. At least my body had the good sense to move all the fat to one location, my stomach, like the doc said. I didn't have a muffin top. I had a portobello mushroom. Of course, that wasn't nearly as interestin' as the mood swings. I had days I'd cry at everything—cats, dogs, birds, children, recognition at work—didn't matter what, I would cry myself silly. Of course, the happy days were more fun. You could've run a car over my foot, and I would've laughed until the cows came home.

One particular day, I was in my angry place. That may sound dangerous, but I had learned right quick to recognize the drug's emotional shifts, and so even though I felt angry, my brain remembered I really shouldn't be. That particular day though I felt a little more ornery than usual. I walked into my boss's office and informed him that he was not to speak to me or I'd punch him in his face.

Of course, my boss looked at me a bit confused. I just looked at him and said, "Angry day, trust me."

He nodded, and I went to work in my cube. I heard my boss sneakin' around the other cubes tellin' folks not to talk to me. That was when I decided I needed to change things up. I'd never liked being the center of attention for very long, and it was making the work environment tense. Sittin' there even on my angry day, I knew we needed some laughs around me.

Now when I talk about being able to see, please don't get me wrong. My sight would come and go, but the medication ensured I could consistently see out of one eye. The doctor had no idea why my eyes seemed to alternate with prednisone, but I was along for the ride. Of course, I never told my coworkers at the time since that sort of thing is hard to explain. Everyone around me just knew I was losin' my eyesight. The tension from my lack of communication, the mood swings, and the constant visual changes was wearin' on folks, especially me.

The mornin' after my angry day, I saw my first opportunity to change the vibes I had been sendin' out. I walked into the breakroom to get my mornin' coffee, and some friends were hangin' out talkin'. They all got quiet when I walked in, unsure what to say or what mood I would be in. In that moment, an epiphany hit me. I realized that goin' blind meant I could tell blind jokes. You know, those jokes everybody tells in the corner of rooms at parties after a few drinks of moonshine. I tried to remember one of the more off-color jokes, and I let her fly.

You could have heard a pin drop. Even with my wonky vision, I could see the terror on people's faces, as they were unsure how to react. That just struck me as so funny. I started a hootin' and hollerin' right there in the break room. I guess everyone else realized I wasn't jokin' out of bitterness, and they all start laughin' too. Pretty soon we had other folks laughin'. From that point on, I would try to come up with at least one inappropriate blind joke a day just to get us all in the right frame of mind.

Of course, I have to admit, not every joke was self-deprecating or even meant to give other people laughs. In fact, my favorite joke was designed to annoy other folks and make me laugh. We had this row of women who didn't like noise. I had heard more noise in a country cemetery at two in the morning than I'd hear walkin' down the hall between their cubicles. To make it worse, if your side of the office raised its noise level too high, these women would come over and fuss at you to keep it down.

Now don't get me wrong. They were good folks. They just wanted it quiet, and I will admit I've gotten on their bad side a few times because I can be a right loud individual. Well, one day I was walkin' by their cubes to get to my side of the office and bumped into the outside wall of a cubicle. That was not an unusual occurrence back in those days as my shiftin' vision would throw me off kilter, and some days it would take my brain a little bit to adjust, makin' me misjudge where my body was. On this particular day, I just happened to bump into the cubicle of one of these women.

Her head popped over that short wall like a prairie dog in the desert. When she saw it was me, she only said, "Oh."

We wished each other good mornin', and I headed on over to my cube. As I was sittin' there, an idea dawned on me. I needed some entertainment, and my idea would not cause anyone any harm. I guess if I'm honest, it did cause me a sore shoulder until my shoulders toughened up.

With my idea firmly implanted, I got up later to grab some coffee from the break room. I headed on back to my cube and made sure I took the silent hallway to get there. I made a point of bumpin' every wall with the shoulder that was not armed with the coffee at the end of it. Sure enough, it was like a whole prairie dog colony. The women popped up their heads one after another, and then a few on the other side joined in when they heard the thump and rustlin'.

I turned at the end of the hallway and apologized. These nice ladies all nodded and told me not to give it another thought. They were sorry to see me bumpin' into walls. I was smilin' when I got back to my cube because I knew I had them hooked. So, when I needed to cheer myself up during the week, I'd take a walk down the hallway of silence and shake things up a mite. I reckon I never did anyone any harm, and who knows, maybe it broke up their otherwise monotonous day.

Now the home front was a different story. Darla had four sons to care for and a husband goin' blind to deal with. I decided she probably could do without my shenanigans. Besides, that was what work was for. I will say that when it comes to my wife I married way up. She has stayed with me through lean and thick times. She has never cheated on me or run away, not even for a little while. Darla's unwaverin' commitment is one of the many things I love about her.

She is also the smartest woman I know. Unfortunately, her high IQ gets in the way of a little common sense from time to time. Like havin' a turkey for a pet, for instance.

As time slid on by, my eyesight got worse. We had been tryin' various drugs to get me off that steroid, and all had some success, but they also had side effects. One drug actually grew all the hair back on my head and helped my eyes. Unfortunately, it also put hair on my back and made my arms so furry that my clothes could not touch my skin. Yet, Darla never complained. Well, she did complain about the sinks gettin' clogged but never about the treatments. Unfortunately, I had to give that drug up on account of a bleedin' ulcer. Sadly, my new head of hair fell out, but son of a gun, my back hair remained. I think some scientist got that backwards.

The kids were good, and we tried to keep the worst information from them. I made a point of watchin' them as much as possible in case I wouldn't get to see them no more. I was talkin' with Darla about the kids and what it might be like one day not to be able to see them. Darla told me I should picture them as I always remember them, and that I could picture her like we looked back in college. I thought that was the smartest idea since sliced bread.

Then Darla's smart brain started askin' me how I'd get around. I will admit, the thought hadn't crossed my mind. I just assumed I'd get one of those white sticks and whack people in the shins as I was shoppin'. Darla's brain started runnin' about a hundred miles an hour with different ideas. She started talkin' about a seein' eye dog, and I told her I didn't know if we had the room for another dog. Our small suburban home at the time was really meant for a family of four, and we had a family of six livin' in it. She then suggested we could get our current pet dog, Belle, trained as a seein' eye dog. Darla pointed out that the dog was a basset, and bassets are smart after all.

Now I don't know if y'all have seen a basset. They are about knee-high to a grasshopper. If you put a basset in front of a blind man and have it stop at an intersection, that blind person is gonna go trippin' over that hound and end up road pizza. Darla was unconvinced, but I simply pulled the blind card, crossed my arms, and told her I would figure it out. Then I burst out laughin' at the thought of our basset tryin' to lead me around.

Things continued to deteriorate, and I made plans to move back to the family farm and live out my life helpin' out where I could, and possibly doing a little preachin'. After all, who is goin' to complain to a blind preacher about his preachin'? I figured the kids would have room to play, and it would lessen the blow of their father losin' his sight.

When I went back to the eye doctor for one of my many visits, we went through our usual routine of dilation and blindin' me with his magnifying glass. Today was a bit different though. When he got done lookin' in my eyes, he threw that magnifyin' lens on the table next to him and started cussin'. Now, I hadn't ever heard a doctor cuss before. I assumed it was somethin' that they weren't allowed to do. He composed himself and let me know my retinas were bleedin'.

I reckoned I knew somethin' had changed on account of my eyes burnin' when light touched them, so I assumed he was right. He went on telling me I would lose my eyesight in less than two weeks, and things wouldn't just be blurry. Everything would go completely black on account of the blood damaging the retina. He said that about two days before I lost my sight it would return to normal right before it all went bad.

Needless to say, that was a long drive home. I had been watching every sunrise and sunset since the drama had begun, but now I got up before dawn and stayed outside after sunset. I had to wear sunglasses all the time due to the pain. Of course, I used the two weeks to pull out a new joke at work. Every time somebody came into my cube, I would imitate either Ray Charles or Stevie Wonder. Somebody mentioned to me one day that I was the wrong color to be doin' that, but I told them when you're blind the color doesn't matter. They just grunted and walked away.

The day finally came when I woke up, and the light no longer hurt my eyes. In fact, they felt fine. In addition, my eyesight was perfect. It was as good as, if not better than, it had been previously. I suppose I should have been a happy fella, but I knew that meant I had two days left. I soaked in every view. I was due to go back to the doctor in less than twenty-four hours. I waited and thought about the prospect of Darla possibly guidin' me in to see the doctor.

The day came to head to the doctor's office, and I could still see. I had Darla go with me, in case things went dark while I was at the office. They called me back, and the doctor got in there pretty quick. He started lookin' at my eyes, shuffled around his notes, and did it again. By the third time, I was gettin' annoyed on account of going half blind every time he stuck that bright light in my direction. The doctor looked over at his papers again and cursed.

Now I was concerned. The last time this happened he told me I would be goin' completely blind. I was startin' to wonder what was worse. I finally asked him what the problem was as he dug through papers for the umpteenth time.

"I did tell you that your retinas were bleeding, right?" he asked me.

I told him yes and reminded him of the pain I was havin' to light. He cocked his head, a smile formed on the ends of his mouth, and then finally started talkin'. "This doesn't make any sense. I have down here your retinas were bleeding, but they are fine now."

I tried to soak in what he was tellin' me. "Is that a problem?"

The doctor kept on shakin' his head in disbelief, "No, but it doesn't make any sense. There should be at least some scarring, but your retinas look brand new. Like newborn new. There isn't a mark on them. There should be something on them for a man your age, but they are perfect."

We both sat there smilin', dumbfounded by the miracle. I finally asked the doctor if he thought it was a miracle.

The doctor cleared his throat and answered, "Officially, I have to put it down a self-regeneration, but just so you know, the body doesn't normally do that."

I was grinnin' ear to ear. He told me to come back in a week. The next few weeks were spent lowering medication and me enjoyin' every sight I could soak in. My disease was not gone, and we still had a fight on our hands, but my eyes had been spared.

Somewhere, among the thousands of people around the globe that were prayin' for me durin' that time, somebody had the faith of a mustard seed and moved my mountain. I would like to take credit for it, but the good Lord knows how I have struggled at times, and I want to avoid bein' struck blind again. Even today, my retinas are younger than the rest of me. So, if you're in need of a miracle, just remember, if God can make a blind moonshinin' hillbilly see, He can answer your prayers too.

BEFUDDLED IN
ST. AUGUSTINE

Now I reckon, if most folks were honest, they'd tell you they have at least one ghost story in their life. Of course, nobody talks much about their brush with the supernatural on account of folks gossipin' around the neighborhood or hollerin' on social media. Let's be honest, we all have that crazy cousin or uncle who has traveled to or lives in some old house and will tell you wild tales of apparitions or things that go bump in the night.

The folks with good sense don't ever talk about such things, not unless it's Halloween or there's a campfire, tents, and small children involved. In those cases, we like to share tales of fantasy and fiction to see if we can get a rise out of somebody. I know I sure do. I will admit, as long as I can remember, such things always fascinated me. I suppose part of this is due to my obsession with mysteries, thrills, and the work of solving a puzzle of unknown origins. I blame Saturday mornin's and *Scooby Doo*.

Then again, it could have somethin' else to do with my childhood. Now, I could blame it on the old farmhouse, the ghost stories, and pranks my older siblin's would play on me, or maybe simply the wild imagination of an elementary school child who stayed up watchin' too much *Night Gallery* at way too young an age. Whatever the reason, my brush with the ethereal plane as a child was not one I enjoyed.

I'd go to sleep, exhausted from a day of school, homework, chores, and play. My little body would sink down into my featherbed. I felt safe in my parent's house because I knew my dad would shoot anything tryin' to come in to hurt us. I always enjoyed fallin' asleep on my stomach with the sheets tucked in around me. There was somethin' reassurin' about bein' snuggled into bed.

However, that all changed one fateful night when I was awakened by somethin' holdin' me to the bed. Of course, I did what any smart child would have done—I squeezed my eyes tight and didn't dare open them. This thing that held me down evidently had a temper, and for some reason, I had triggered it. It held me there tellin' me how it was going to kill me. Although I was just knee-high to a grasshopper, I knew exactly what to do. I hollered for my mama. I didn't dare wake my daddy up since he had to go to work in a few hours.

Momma came rushin' into my room and flipped on the light. As soon as she did, I could move. Of course, I sat there and cried. Unlike those heartless parents on television, my momma didn't tell me to go back to sleep and turn off the light. Instead, she took me to their bed. This game of ghostly threats and rescues from my mom went on for years. I'll give it to the specter, he was persistent. When I got too big to sleep in Momma and Daddy's double bed, Momma stayed in my room until I fell asleep. On the nights she didn't feel up to sittin' with me, I would sneak into my brother's room and sleep with him.

I reckon you could say I didn't sleep much growin' up. Lookin' back on my childhood, I could blame these episodes on my vivid imagination and young age, except the ill spirit never did stop. He kept on harassin' me all the way up through my teen years until I moved away. I suppose he was annoyed that he never got a chance to kill me, unless he had intended to do it with insomnia. One of the last nights I spent in that haunted room was the worst.

I had avoided some of the phantom's visits by firmly planting myself on my side at night. I figured it was harder for him to hold me down in that position, and that seemed to be the case. He stayed away for a couple of years until I was sixteen.

A scratchin' noise roused me out of my sleep one night. Bein' a teenager, it took me a few seconds to get my bearin's. At first, I thought I was comin' out of some dream, but then the scratches got louder. Dad didn't allow critters to get anywhere near the house, so I doubted mice or any other animals could have possibly gotten into the walls. Bein' a gangly teenager, full of vim and vigor, I did what any other boy my age would have done. I threw the covers over my head.

I peeked out from underneath the cotton-filled comforter towards my red nightlight. There, against the red-hued wall, was the shadow of what looked like a demon. Of course, I have no idea what those really look like, but it looked like a cross between a dragon and a man. I never asked myself if it could be a combination of my record player and furniture creatin' a shadow on the wall. I suppose that never occurred to me on account of the familiar angry voice I could hear.

He seemed especially annoyed on this particular night. He growled, hissed, and told me I was dead. The scratchin' got worse, and I wrestled with hollerin' for my mom. After all, sixteen-year-old boys don't holler for their momma. After what seemed like a couple more minutes, I threw caution to the wind and hollered. This time, both my parents came into the room. I suppose they took the shrieks of a sixteen-year-old a little more seriously than a six-year-old. When I told them what had happened, my father said he'd check for mice. I got out of bed and checked around my room. Everythin' was normal.

My folks went back to bed, and I stayed awake the rest of the night. Needless to say, I have developed more than a healthy respect for things that go bump in the night. After I moved out of that house, all the harassment stopped. When I accepted Jesus' free gift of salvation, I started goin' to church and talked to folks about my haunted room. Most told me it was in my mind on account of there not bein' any such thing as ghosts.

However, the older I got, the more I realized those folks really hadn't read much of the large Bible they liked to lug into church every Sunday mornin'. There are all sorts of stories about folks talkin' to the dead, demons possessin' all sorts of people, and even Jesus bein' mistaken for a specter. I will say the good book did show me that I had nothin' to fear because God is watchin' over us, but more importantly, it showed me that I wasn't crazy. With my mind at peace, I put those days behind me. I figured as long as I watched myself, I would be okay.

I was right, at least until I dated this one girl while in college. Of course, young love was involved. This young woman's name was Chrissy. Her family hailed from eastern North Carolina, and she taught me all sorts of interestin' things about that part of the state back in the 1980s. The time period is important because back then that part of the state was extremely poor. Cotton had been banned on account of the boll weevil. With the soil that was available, the only thing most folks grew was peanuts or tobacco. As you can imagine, you can't make much of a livin' on peanuts.

With so much poverty, most homesteads were worn down or downright shabby. Of course, with old dreary houses come tales of ghosts, especially since most of the entertainment came from the family musicians or the neighborhood storytellers. So, I wasn't too surprised by the stories when I got to meet her grandfather, a much older gentleman, who lived in a house that had been built around the 1700s. The family had helped him keep the house up, so it didn't look nearly as spooky as some of the dwellin's just down the road.

The inside of this house was a sight to behold. It had a staircase so old that it rose along the side of the wall without any railin'. I suppose folks back then figured that if you fell off you probably didn't have the good sense or coordination to survive the harsh conditions back in the eighteenth century. The house's heating had been accomplished through multiple fireplaces. Since Chrissy's grandfather was very old, these had all been neglected in favor of space heaters. Needless to say, our visit on this particular January was pretty chilly inside the confines of this historic home.

My college roommate and I stayed in a room downstairs on twin beds and my girlfriend and her roommate stayed up yonder in the upstairs bedroom. Given that we were in college, that was probably a smart arrangement. So, as my roommate, Patrick, and I got ready for bed, the girls snuck into the room to tell us goodnight.

Now, one of the things I liked about Chrissy was her sense of humor. She was very similar to me and didn't mind gettin' a rise out of somebody. So when she sat down on the edge of the bed and told me that the house was haunted, I laughed her off, at first.

Chrissy insisted that the room right above ours held a spirit that frightened them as children by movin' the furniture around. She had shown us the room earlier in the day. I will note that her grandfather had acquired several beautiful antique pieces over his long lifetime. However, there wasn't nothin' movin' in that room since you could hardly walk inside it due to all the pieces fillin' up the place. Of course, somewhere in the back of my head, those memories of my childhood surfaced, but I didn't say nothin'. After all, I didn't want to become that crazy uncle.

The girls left for bed, and Patrick and I laughed about Chrissy's ghost story. We both spent a little time readin' our Bibles before goin' on to sleep, but of course, that was on account of our devotion to the Lord, not because we were scared. I reckoned we hadn't been asleep long when we heard the door to the room creak open. I knew I wasn't imaginin' somethin' on account of Patrick whisperin' to me, askin' me if I heard the door. About that time, a bright ball of light filled that old room. I squealed like my cousin whenever she would get chased around the yard with a garden snake, not that I know anythin' about that.

Behind the ball of light came the familiar giggles of Chrissy and her roommate, Michelle. The giggles alternated between shushin' and laughter. Needless to say, Patrick and I were not amused. Chrissy came on over and gave me a hug and a kiss, and all the animus that I was feelin' melted away. With a second goodnight, Patrick and I laid back down. We had just about fallen asleep when a scrapin' noise from the ceilin' caught our attention.

Patrick and I whispered back and forth, askin' each other over and over if the other was hearin' what we were hearin'. At this point, I was startin' to have flashbacks to my childhood and debatin' crawlin' into bed with my roommate, not really considerin' how that might be perceived as a bit awkward. Fortunately, Patrick had a better frame of mind and brought up the idea of the girls tryin' to scare us again. I debated Chrissy goin' in there at night on account of her childhood, but then it occurred to me that the whole thing had been a ruse.

Patrick and I both agreed it was one of the best practical jokes we had fallen victims to and then fell fast asleep.

The next January mornin' was cold in the old house, and we were thankful to head over to the warm, brick dwelling of her uncle's house next door for breakfast. When the girls asked us how we slept, we both smiled at each other, and then the girls. We told them we had a great night's sleep after they had left the room. The girls both seemed annoyed. Patrick and I were pleased with ourselves because we thought we had spoiled the girls' joke.

After breakfast, we packed up the car and piled inside for the drive back to college. For the first twenty minutes, the car was silent, and you could feel the tension between the girls and us. I finally spoke up since nobody was talkin'.

"What're y'all so sore about?" I asked.

Chrissy shot back, "You kept us awake all night with your knockin'."

Her answer surprised me. After all, I had expected her to say she was mad that we didn't hear them movin' around the furniture. A thought crossed my mind that it could be an attempt to salvage their haunted joke by claimin' somethin' was knockin' on their door. I decided to end the charade.

I looked at both girls as I spoke, "I don't know how anyone could be knockin' on your door when y'all were busy slidin' the furniture around our heads."

The car got quiet, and you could feel the tension disappear. The expression on Chrissy and Michelle's face told me right away that they hadn't pulled any pranks.

Chrissy spoke barely above a whisper, "We didn't move any furniture. In fact, we never left our room after we scared you boys."

The four of us looked back and forth at each other as the old blue Chevy Impala went barrellin' down the flat country road.

"Really?" was all I could think of askin'.

The two girls nodded, and Patrick and I looked at each other, unable to hide our shock. It was at that moment that I had a major epiphany. Not every phantom was out to kill you. In fact, there really is an entire other creation beyond our limited world of space and time. The longer I live, the more I read my Bible, and the more I get to know folks, the more I am convinced that this world is a pale reflection of the world the Almighty has already made for us. Our eternity isn't in our future; we are surrounded by it. The problem is, we are too busy staring at the hand in front of our face to notice the wonders and terrors all around us.

This understandin' don't make such encounters any less frightenin'. Just like bein' surrounded by a pack of coyotes, findin' yourself in a presence of a demon will still put your life in peril. Shoot, even when angels show up, folks get spooked. There ain't any place in the Bible where an angel appears, and folks simply say, "Hey, how y'all doin'?" Every time one of those bein's make a sudden appearance, folks are freakin' out, and the angel is tellin' them to calm on down. I'm surprised they don't carry along a mason jar for folks to sip on to help relax their nerves.

My newfound knowledge hasn't really squelched my fascination with the other side none. I have to admit, if anything, it has stoked it hotter than ethanol on a bonfire. I am always up for an adventure or seein' things most folks only see on television, so if I have an opportunity to experience it firsthand, I head on out and take advantage of the opportunity. So, when Darla said she wanted to stop in St. Augustine on our way to the Florida Keys for our wedding anniversary, I was all for it.

St. Augustine is the oldest continuously inhabited city in the United States. It was founded in 1565 by Spain. I realize the British like to pretend they somehow founded the "colonies," but Spain showed up in the new world second, after the Vikings. The British were a distant third and didn't even have the good sense to look for the warmer land. I reckon havin' your home country in the North Atlantic makes places like Maryland feel tropical. St. Augustine is also known as one of the most haunted cities in the United States, mostly due to its age. It also has the distinction of being the location of the Fountain of Youth. At least, that's what the late Juan Ponce de Leon thought.

The tourist trap I was most intrigued with down yonder was its lighthouse. When I would get done with a day's work, I used to love to come home at night and watch *Ghost Hunters* whenever they were on the television. At least in the early years of the show, Jason and Grant did a good job of provin' bumps as nothin' but bumps. So, you knew when they couldn't debunk somethin', they had found a real spook. Of course, later on those poor boys seemed to find ghosts in all sorts of places, and many times they simply weren't there. However, their crownin' achievement was the St. Augustine lighthouse.

They had managed to capture a shadow of a figure in the empty lighthouse with nothing more than a camera sittin' on a tripod. The shadowy man seemed to leap from one level to the next in a mere second. Finally, at the top, the black figure appeared to be holding a lantern while lookin' over the rail down towards the floor where the video camera sat on its stand. Multiple sources validated nobody was in that lighthouse, not even the *Ghost Hunters* crew, at the time of the shadow man. Needless to say, this lighthouse was on my list of places I wanted to see if I ever had the chance.

Darla has always been the kind of woman who finds unknown facts about esoteric people and places that are often forgotten about or overlooked. I reckon that trait has somethin' to do with the reason she married me. So, when Darla asked to take point on accommodations in St. Augustine, I was all for handin' that responsibility over to her. She did not disappoint. When our car pulled into the parking lot of the Holiday Inn, I found she had planted us within walking distance of every old town tourist spot.

The hotel showed its age inside, and I reckoned that was from the humidity and mold that appeared to be winning the battle against the establishment. The hotel room was clean and respectable though. On our first day in the old haunted city, we decided to walk over and eat dinner at a Denny's located next door. I was a mite concerned that there were very few patrons, but we were eatin' at four-thirty in the afternoon since we had traveled most of the day to get there. It had been a long time since I had been to a Denny's, and I have to be honest, I had not missed a thing. That food was about as common as grits with salt.

Right behind our hotel was San Marco Street. Darla explained to me that we could walk along this road to find everything we were looking for. As evening began to fall, we thought we would check out the local church of the Shrine of Lady of La Leche at Mission Nombre De Dios directly behind us. The church was founded in 1565 and featured an amazing two-hundred-foot cross that we could see from almost anywhere we went durin' our visit. There was a beautiful pond and grounds surroundin' the church.

As I was admirin' the grounds, I noticed a very old cemetery on the other side of the facility. I started gettin' excited. There is somethin' about standing around a bunch of old dust and bones from hundreds of years ago that makes me feel like I'm touchin' history. I guess it shouldn't be no surprise the dearly departed would follow me around.

They are probably angry with me for wakin' them up. Unfortunately, everything was locked up tight. Evidently, you had to have permission to wander about the old grounds.

On the other side of the property, the church was holdin' a huge celebration. It looked like every person within a twenty-mile circumference had come for the shindig. There were carnival rides all over the facility, as well as pony rides and what appeared to be small contests in some of the booths. Children laughed and played, and even the parents were smilin'. Darla and I walked over to one of the quieter areas of the sprawlin' campus and soaked in the vibe of the good Lord's love among the people. We found us a bench, sat down, and in front of the two-hundred-foot cross, I contemplated my life and how I might be able to get around the fencin' into the cemetery. After people watchin' for a bit, we turned in.

The next mornin', Darla suggested we go visit the Fountain of Youth. Now, my folks had visited it when they were newly married, and I felt like it was my obligation, and privilege, to follow in their footsteps. The entrance to the facility had a rather convincin' statue of Juan Ponce De Leon. I took a picture of Darla lookin' a bit too comfortable hangin' onto the statue's arm.

Once we paid and went inside, the grounds sprawled out and backed up to the church. Although we were closer to that cemetery, I still could not find a way in, at least not without gettin' into some serious trouble. The fabled fountain of youth was well hidden with large signs every few feet invitin' tourist into a long building where the spring resided. Once we got past all the small statues that played out the drama of the settlers takin' their first sip of the famed spring, we finally made it to the water's source. I was somewhat disappointed by the water that flowed across what appeared to be a manmade creek and into a pipe that then released it to a drain. Disposable cups invited all who would come to partake. Seein' that it would be a wasted trip if we didn't drink, Darla and I both took us a good swig.

Lawd have mercy, I ain't tasted sulfur like that since Yellowstone Park. Darla and I threw the cups away and debated regurgitating the water, but we figured that wasn't a neighborly thing to do. The rest of that mornin' was nothin' more than a series of swollen bellies, cramps, and a battle between gettin' our money's worth around the historical park and runnin' back to the hotel for the bathroom.

After an hour or so of grittin' our teeth and clenchin' our cheeks, we made our way back to the hotel as quickly as possible. After an hour or so of sweet relief at the hotel, we left and saw the other landmarks, such as Castillo de San Marcos, and the nearby conglomeration of stores and restaurants. We were plumb bushed, but I still had not seen the site I wanted to see the most.

I broke out the folder in the hotel that showed all of the tourist traps, and I found several ghost tours, but none of them allowed tourist to actually tour the old lighthouse at night. I finally found the Dark of the Moon Tour. It was the perfect choice. Not only would we get to tour the lighthouse in the dark, we would get the run of the place for forty-five minutes of unsupervised ghost hunting. I called and made the arrangements. I was sore, exhausted, and could not wait to finally see the spook that had been made so famous by cable TV.

Arrivin' at the lighthouse really set the mood. In the dark, the parkin' lot was almost impossible to see, as it was nestled in a grove of trees. The facilities were old with lots of creakin' old hinges, swollen wood, and chipped paint around different parts of the complex. Two very nice young ladies led us on our ghost tour. I must admit, they had my hair raised on the back of my neck with some of their tales of hauntin' from within the light keeper's home as well as the lighthouse.

As we climbed up the black iron steps of the lighthouse, I could easily imagine how hard it must have been to climb the summit multiple times a day with fuel for the light. About halfway up the stairs, I stopped. I would be seein' dead people soon if I didn't catch my breath. As I sat there, I hoped the shadow man would appear on the banister near me. I wanted to know what he thought of death as a celebrity, but unfortunately, he did not seem inclined to interact with us tourists.

Darla and I finally made it to the top, and as I walked out on the terrace that surrounded the lighthouse, I gasped in fear. I'm terrified of heights. Darla laughed and walked around me. I forced myself out onto the circular terrace by pullin' up my camera and snappin' photos of the city lights twinklin' below in the shadows of the night. I walked back inside feelin' scared but not seein' any ghosts.

Darla and I made it back down the stairs and out into the courtyard. I noticed a lot of folks were sittin' outside enjoyin' the snacks they had bought from the snack bar. I wasn't hungry, and to be honest, at this point, I felt pulled back towards the keeper's house. At first, I was goin' to ask Darla to join me, but somethin' had me feelin' afraid. It could have been residual fear from our climb up the lighthouse summit, but every fiber in my body told me to bring other folks.

I approached two couples that were sittin' on the house steps to see if they would join us in the basement where a certain ghost was supposed to reside. I reckoned they were like me because they were all for goin' right back in as a group, but none of them seemed inspired to return to the dark, quiet basement on their own. While the group got themselves together, Darla and I entered the main floor to do a quick walk through with my phone recordin' sound.

My butt cheeks tightened up as we entered the home, and I made my way to the room that the workers all said they refused to enter due to sinister shadow figures that would appear there. I will be the first to say that it was very creepy. Period furniture passed by the flashlights on our phone. Their muted colors crossed across our field of vision like a scene straight out of *Supernatural*. I forced my way through the room, wishin' I had Wobbly with me. Darla had lagged behind to admire the period furniture. I stopped as the path dead-ended inside a sealed hallway. Although there was only a thermostat on the wall, that part of the house felt most foreboding. I chalked it up to my nerves.

I turned back, met up with Darla, and we headed for the basement. Most of the folks who had promised to return were already millin' about the room. There was an older woman sittin' in a folding chair in the middle of the room where the ghost is said to interact with tourists. As I stood against the wall, I bumped up against another patron. However, when I turned to apologize, there weren't nobody there. That got my attention, and I stood there with my voice recorder, hopin' I might pick somethin' up, like a ghost sayin', "Excuse me." After all, that's the polite thing to do.

After a few minutes, my legs, worn out from the day's events, demanded I sit down. So, I sat in the chair next to the older woman. I reckoned my rude friend was floatin' around the walls, so I would not be bothered in the middle of the room. A minute after I sat down, the nice woman sittin' next to me joked that she wanted the ghost to rub her leg. I don't mind sharin' that made me feel a might uncomfortable. I was afraid the ghost would either take her up on her offer or possibly feel insulted. The air in the room turned warm and heavy. So much so, that everyone commented on it. We all got quiet, but nothin' happened.

I looked around for Darla and noticed she had walked over towards the indoor cisterns. The tour guide warned us not to try and climb in as people had gotten stuck in there. In fact, accordin' to the guide, the heavy bald fella from *Ghost Hunters* had gotten stuck inside after bein' told not to go in. That got me to wonderin' if those boys were even plumbers. After all, if a plumber can't climb in and out of a cistern, who can? I walked on over, and Darla was there talkin' into the cistern, asking some unseen critter to give her a sign. I felt myself tense up because I was concerned they might grant her request.

At that point, I noticed the compass on Darla's iPhone 6S begin to slowly spin one direction and then the other. At first I thought it was runnin' some sort of calibration program because it would stop for a second and start up again. But after a few seconds, it started spinnin' like a top so fast you couldn't make out any of the markin's. I commented to Darla that there was somethin' goin' on with her phone, and she told me she had been watchin' it too. I asked to see it and began scannin' around our location.

Now, I know computers and electronics, and it seems obvious that there had to be an electrical field interfering with the compass's sensors. However, every time I put the phone anywhere near an electrical outlet, conduit, and or anything of that nature, the spinning stopped. It also only spun at certain heights near the cistern and well away from any power sources. Whatever it was, it seemed content to follow me around a couple other parts of the basement as I continued to try and debunk what I was experiencin'.

The air in the room was mighty heavy, and it seemed obvious to me that there was somethin' in the room with us. However, I didn't feel afraid like I had as a child. I reckoned that could have been due to Darla standing right next to me. We wandered on upstairs and the spinnin' stopped. We walked back outside, and I turned off my audio recorder, debating what to do next. I decided to head on over to the woman who had given us the tour and tell her what happened. She seemed unsurprised and said she was happy we were able to experience somethin' as there are no guarantees. I guess it depends on how sociable the ghosts are feelin'.

By this point, Darla and my joints were beginin' to feel their arthritis, but the issues with the compass nagged on me. I wanted to know if Darla's phone was broken or if there was somethin' in that house. Everyone was now out of the house, so I asked the guide if she would take Darla and me back inside to get a second reading to compare what we heard. The nice worker agreed, and the three of us went inside. Everything had completely changed. The air was cool and light, and at first, I thought it might be the air conditioner, but nothin' was blowin'. We walked around the basement. The uneven wooden floor that was used to simulate a ship's deck and its smooth walls held nothing to bump up against me. In fact, everything felt so normal as to be boring. We walked around with the phone's compass. Nothing spun, and it acted as designed. Even the creepy room on the main floor felt altogether normal and empty.

We left the house happy. We knew that whatever had happened had not been something in the environment. At this point, Darla and I were both exhausted and decided to head back to the hotel. We rested our sore and worn bodies upon the hotel bed. I decided I would wait until morning to check the recordings. After all, we had seen the compass with our own eyes, and I had been bumped. Once more, I felt inspired by the mysteries of God's creation.

I woke up long before Darla the next mornin'. Actually, that's an event that happens every mornin'. After wakin' up, I sat quietly with my headphones on and listened to the recordin' from the night before. I could close my eyes and see every room and footstep we had taken in the darkened old lighthouse keeper's house. I heard the folding chair groan as I sat down in it. We all laughed at the old women asking the ghost to touch her thigh, and then a long, low, harmonic moan passed through my earbuds. I sat up and looked around the hotel room. Only the small sunbeam escaping through the crack of the curtains pierced the darkness.

I backed up the audio and heard it again. I let the recordin' continue to play. As I commented about Darla's spinnin' compass, I heard the moan again. I smiled as I imagined this poor spectre having an older woman tell him to rub her legs, and it letting out a despondent moan in response. Next, he had tried to leave with me. He set off the compass to try and communicate, and the best response he could garner from an old country boy was my obsession with the electronics. Was it any wonder he had let out such laments into my phone's microphone? He was probably the same fella that bumped me in the shoulder tryin' to get my attention. I reckon those spirits think we mortals are mighty thick.

As Darla and I left St. Augustine for the Florida Keys, it got me to reflectin' on that ornery spirit from my childhood. There are certainly created bein's out there that mean to do us harm. However, much like lions, wolves, housecats, and dogs, there are unknown creatures that simply want to talk to us, to be recognized. Who knows, maybe they're old Spaniards, lighthouse keepers, children whose lives were cut short, or possibly somethin' altogether different. I reckon we miss a lot of the good Lord's creation with our hustle, bustle, and distractions.

The next time you find yourself out in the woods huntin', next to a lake fishin', or perhaps visitin' an old homestead, just stand or sit and listen. There could be somethin' whisperin' your name or touching your arm, maybe even tappin' your shoulder. Perhaps the Almighty is goin' to show you the beauties, mysteries, and terrors of his creation you've been missin'. Y'all be good.

www.ingramcontent.com/pod-product-compliance
Lightning Source LLC
Chambersburg PA
CBHW030215130726
47898CB00012B/1035